Harlequin
Presents..

Other titles by

ANNE MATHER
IN HARLEQUIN PRESENTS

75c each

Many of these titles, and other titles in the Harlequin Romance series, are available at your local bookseller, or through the Harlequin Reader Service. For a free catalogue listing all available Harlequin Presents titles and Harlequin Romances, send your name and address to:

HARLEQUIN READER SERVICE,
M.P.O. Box 707
Niagara Falls, N.Y. 14302

Canadian address:
Stratford, Ontario, Canada
or use order coupon at back of books.

ANNE MATHER

legacy of the past

HARLEQUIN BOOKS
toronto-winnipeg

© Anne Mather 1966

First published in 1966 under the title "Beloved Stranger"

Mills & Boon edition published 1973

SBN 373-70557-3
Harlequin Presents edition published August 1974

Printed in Canada.

CHAPTER ONE

MADELINE folded the last letter and placed it in the envelope, sealing it thankfully. There; she was finished!

She pulled the plastic cover over her typewriter, locked her drawer and slipped the keys into her shopping bag. Walking to the door she lifted down her sheepskin coat and put it on, surveying the room as she did so to satisfy herself that everything was tidied up for the week-end. Then, satisfied, she opened the door and stepped into the corridor outside.

The long, rubber-tiled corridors stretched away ahead of her, flanked by classrooms and more corridors. Deserted now, without the chattering throng of boys and girls, it looked stark and uninspiring.

Suddenly the figure of George Jackson, the school porter, appeared from around one of the many corners and made his way towards her. Madeline smiled at his approach, liking the elderly custodian who looked after things so efficiently.

'Not away yet, Mrs. Scott?' he asked, as he neared her. 'It's past five o'clock, you know.'

Madeline nodded. 'I'm just going, George. I've left the last few letters on my desk, as usual.'

'All right, I'll see to them.' George searched his pockets for his pipe. 'You get along now, my dear. That daughter of yours will be wondering where you are.'

'You may be right,' said Madeline, smiling again. 'See you on Monday.'

She walked away down the corridor, her heels almost soundless on the rubber flooring. Although it was empty the school still had appeal for her. She enjoyed working there as secretary to Adrian Sinclair, the headmaster. She had been his secretary for over five years now, ever since they came to Otterbury, in fact.

The staff entrance opened on to the school car-park.

5

Madeline, who owned a scooter, left it here and she walked quickly across to where it was parked, the only machine left on the car-park. As she kicked the starter she shivered. Although it was late March, the air was still icily cold in the mornings and evenings, and riding the scooter was not as much fun as it had been during the warm summer months.

She rode to the exit and slowed as she reached the main road. Traffic streamed by, mostly workmen leaving the nearby automobile factory. Although Otterbury was only a small town, the big new factory which had recently sprung up on its outskirts had enlarged the population considerably and new council houses were gradually being built to house the men who at present commuted from further afield.

She turned into the main stream when there was a break in the traffic and changing gear she increased her speed easily. She enjoyed the feeling of freedom the scooter gave her and the menacing vehicles which swarmed past her did not bother her a jot. She was not nervous, she never had been about driving, and riding the scooter took little effort.

Suddenly an enormous red car sped past her, its smooth, snake-like body a sure indication of unlimited speed. Madeline grimaced as the draught of its passing affected her like swell on the ocean and she was hardly righted again before she had to apply her brakes for all she was worth as the tail of the monster seemed to be hurtling at her. The driver had halted abruptly, twin brake lights like beacons illuminating the road even in daylight.

Madeline was too close. She put both feet to the ground tentatively, but the scooter was skidding and a second later she hit the rear of the other vehicle. It was not a severe bump. Her brakes had saved her that, but the scooter overturned and she landed in the road, feeling foolishly like a schoolgirl falling from her cycle.

As she attempted to scramble to her feet two strong hands assisted her, while a voice like crushed ice demanded: 'Whatever do you think you're doing?'

Madeline's eyes widened, and she gazed up at the man confronting her so angrily. Was he actually blaming her? Why, he was the one to blame!

'This is a highway, not a child's playground!' he continued relentlessly, his tone uncompromising. 'You ought to think ahead. Or stay off the road altogether,' he added, as an afterthought.

'Now, wait a minute,' began Madeline indignantly. 'It was your fault for stopping so precipitately.' She fumed as sardonic eyes surveyed her, and she wondered what nationality he really was. There was a faint but unmistakable accent in his voice that was definitely not English. 'This road was not built for motor racing, and cars usually signify their intentions to give their followers forewarning—'

'I am aware of that,' he interrupted her. 'All right, I admit I did stop abruptly, but if I hadn't something much more serious could have happened. If you will walk round to the front of the car you'll see for yourself.'

Straightening her shoulders, even though she felt a little shaky, Madeline walked slowly round the red monster. Then she halted, thrusting her hands into the pockets of her coat. Three vehicles were in collision in the centre of the road, a lorry and two cars, one of which had obviously run into the other two. A police car came whining up the road from Otterbury as she stood there, but happily no one seemed seriously injured.

'Well?' said her companion, looking rather amused now. 'Does that convince you that my motives were reasonable?'

Madeline shrugged. 'Of course. I'm sorry I was so quick to jump to conclusions, but really, a scooter doesn't have the braking power of a car like this.' She indicated the automobile.

The man inclined his head. Then he said, rather belatedly: 'Are you hurt?'

Madeline could not suppress a smile. 'No,' she replied, shaking her head. 'I'm all in one piece, thank you. You'd better examine your car. It's much more likely to be in need of repair.'

He smiled too, rather mockingly, and Madeline found herself thinking what an attractive man he was. Tall, with broad shoulders tapering to slim hips, he was very tanned, and his eyes were a dark blue. His hair was very dark as well, and it was this that made Madeline think he might be a Spaniard, or an Italian. He moved with an easy fluid grace of movement and his attitude of indolence seemed to conceal a leashed vitality. The cut of his suit was impeccable and had obviously been made by a master craftsman, and the faint accent and his excellent grasp of English seemed to point to an expensive education. She wondered who he could be. She knew by sight most of the affluent people in Otterbury, but this man was a stranger. And, as though aware of her thoughts, he said:

'As I am attached to the Sheridan factory, I hardly think we need concern ourselves with the repair of my car. Besides, it's only slightly dented, as you can see.'

Sheridans was the car factory further up the road, an Italian–American concern, this being their first enterprise in England. That also seemed to explain his accent. He was obviously of Italian descent, but had probably spent many years in the States.

'That's all right, then,' she said, bending to pick up the scooter and her shopping bag, which was fortunately closed. The man forestalled her, however, lifting the scooter effortlessly and scanning it with a practised eye.

'Your scooter seems to be intact,' he said. 'If anything should go wrong just give us a ring and I'll arrange to have it fixed. The number is Otterbury 2001.'

Madeline thanked him, conscious now of how dishevelled she must appear. As he handed her the scooter she was overwhelmingly conscious of his eyes appraising her quite openly and she felt her cheeks grow hot with embarrassment.

'Th . . . thank you,' she stammered, and kicked the starter. To her relief it started first time and she sat astride

8

the seat and said: 'Good-bye.'

'Au revoir . . . Miss . . . Miss . . .?' He smiled and waited for her answer.

'It's Mrs. Scott,' she corrected him, and with a brief smile she rode away. She was aware of his eyes watching her as she rode down the road, and she prayed she would make no more mistakes.

Within seconds he sped past her, his hand lifted in acknowledgment, and she felt herself relax again.

Reaching the centre of Otterbury she turned right at the traffic lights towards Highnook. Highnook was a suburb of Otterbury where a lot of new housing had gone up, including the block of flats where Madeline lived with her daughter, Diana. The flats were in Evenwood Gardens, overlooking the River Otter, and Madeline always felt a thrill of pleasure when she reached her home. It was such a nice flat and Otterbury was such a pleasant town.

The flat was on the first floor, and as she opened the door and entered the small hallway, she called:

'Diana! Are you home?'

There was no reply, so she closed the door and removed her coat. The living-room opened off the hallway. It was a large room with plain distempered walls which Madeline had ornamented with several plaques. The wall-to-wall carpeting, which had taken a lot of saving for, was sapphire blue, while the three-piece suite was white leather hung with dark blue fringed chair-backs. The heating was all electric, unfortunately, for Madeline preferred an open fire in at least one room. She now turned up the valve which operated the radiators, for although the room was warm compared to the cold air outside it was by no means comfortably so. The room had a homely, lived-in atmosphere. A china cabinet contained her few pieces of really good china and glass and the rest of the space was filled with bookshelves, well filled with novels, a television, and Diana's pick-up which stood on a table in an alcove with a stack of 'pop' records beside it.

Madeline lit a cigarette and turned on the television.

She had shopped at lunchtime and the chops she had bought for their dinner would not take much cooking.

Carrying her shopping bag through to the kitchen which opened off the lounge and was very tiny, she unpacked the food and put on the kettle. Then she returned to the lounge. It was nearly six, so Diana ought not to be long.

She walked into the bedroom which she and Diana shared. There was only one bedroom with a small bathroom and closet adjoining it. The flats were really only intended for one person, but as the two-bedroomed flats had been two pounds more a week, Madeline had had to content herself with the single bedroom. She did not mind for herself, but Diana was getting to an age when she objected to not having a room of her own. However, when they arrived in Otterbury after Joe's death, Madeline had been grateful enough of a place of their own.

She stripped off her jersey dress and went into the bathroom to wash and brush her teeth. As she did so, she found herself wondering what the man in the car had really thought about her. She had found him immensely attractive, but then any woman would. She wondered how old he was. He had only looked to be in his early thirties and as she herself was thirty-three, he was probably about her age.

Brushing her hair, which when loosed from the French knot she usually wore it in fell to her shoulders, she wondered how old he had taken her for. She knew she did not really look her age. Adrian Sinclair was incessantly telling her that she looked more like Diana's sister than her mother, but Adrian wanted to marry her and that was his way.

Of course, Diana grumbled sometimes too, that Madeline wore clothes which were not in keeping with her position as the headmaster's secretary, and a respectable widow, but again, Diana was old-fashioned in some ways. She supposed that was due in some measure to Joe's influence.

Critically, she decided that her eyes were her best feature, greenish-grey with tawny lights and her hair was silky-soft and the colour of rich amber. She was tall; too tall, she always thought, although at least she was nicely rounded and not angular. All in all, she reflected, she was an average, presentable female, but certainly not outstanding in any way.

Now the man, she sighed, he had been outstanding, in every way. She felt sure that dozens of women must have thought so too. After all, in his income bracket, if women were rather dull or drab, their beauty parlour, hair-stylist and plastic surgeon could soon remedy that. From the rather world-weary cynicism she had seen round his eyes and his mouth, he was all too bored with his life and well aware of his own magnetism.

Madeline grimaced at herself in the mirror, amused at her own thoughts. Good heavens, she was behaving like a child, simply because she had happened to meet a man who without question was way out of her sphere!

She slipped her arms into a quilted housecoat and as she buttoned it she pushed all thoughts of the man out of her mind. No matter how she felt, Diana was always her first consideration. Poor Diana, who after all had never really recovered from the shock of losing Joe when she was just seven years old.

As she merged from the bedroom, a key in the lock heralded the arrival of her daughter. Diana breezed in cheerfully enough, a slender, younger edition of Madeline except that her hair was dark brown. Diana was sixteen, and at the commercial college in Otterbury. She was often late home at present as the college was rehearsing for its end of term play and Diana had a starring role. They were performing a play written by another of the students and it was to be staged in the college hall with the proceeds going to local charities.

Diana was not as tall as Madeline and wore her hair fashionably long. Dressed in a dark grey duffel coat and swinging a tartan bag, she was a typical teenager.

'Hello, Mum,' she greeted Madeline, flinging her bag on to a chair. 'Isn't it cold tonight? I'm freezing!'

Madeline nodded. 'Yes, it's not much like spring,' she agreed. 'Did you have a good rehearsal?'

'So-so,' replied Diana, indifferently. 'Miss Hawkes always tries to run the affair like a military tattoo, but apart from that it was all right. It seems such an uproar I'm sure it will never come right.'

Madeline chuckled. 'It will on the night, I'm sure. Never mind, it will soon be over. Term ends in three weeks, doesn't it?'

'Yes, thank goodness. Gosh, then we'll have two whole weeks with nothing to do! It will be glorious!'

Madeline smiled and went into the kitchen. As she prepared the vegetables and put the chops under the grill she decided not to say anything to Diana about falling off the scooter. After all, no harm had been done and Diana often said that Madeline ought to use the bus during peak traffic hours. Diana was a little possessive about her mother at times, probably due to the fact that she was her only relative, and Madeline did not want to cause her any more worry.

They had their dinner in the lounge. One end had been converted into a dining recess by the addition of a velvet curtain, shielding the table from view. Diana set the table while Madeline dished up the meal and they sat together afterwards, idly watching the television while Madeline had a cigarette with her coffee.

'Shall I wash up?' asked Diana, stretching lazily. 'Is Uncle Adrian coming round tonight?'

'I think Adrian's coming and I should be grateful if you would do the washing up. I want to change into something more suitable.'

Diana smiled and rose to her feet and Madeline looked at her queryingly.

'Are ... are you going out tonight?' she asked tentatively.

'Why, yes. Jeff asked me to go to the Seventies Club.'

'Oh!' Madeline nodded.

'Do you mind?'

Madeline ran a tongue over her lips. 'No. No. Why

should I?'

'No reason, but I've noticed you don't really enthuse about my going out with him.'

Madeline half-smiled. 'I'm sorry, darling. Of course you must go.'

Diana shrugged. 'Well, it's something to do,' she said lightly.

'Yes. Besides, Adrian will probably be round later. He said he had some marking to do, but I guess he'll find time,' Madeline smiled wryly.

'He always finds time for you,' murmured Diana slyly.

Madeline compressed her lips. 'Yes, that may be so. But that means nothing, Diana, absolutely nothing.'

Diana shrugged regretfully and began carrying the dishes through to the kitchen. Madeline stubbed out her cigarette in the ashtray and walked through to the bedroom. She was becoming a little tired of Diana's insinuations about herself and Adrian. Truthfully they were insinuations based on fact, but Madeline had no wish to make insinuations reality.

As she dressed in dark blue stretch slacks and an Italian silk over-blouse, she found herself wishing, not for the first time, that Joe was still alive. Diana was growing up now and becoming quite a responsibility in many ways. Also, she had worshipped Joe and he had adored her. He had been a bachelor for so many years before he married Madeline and he had found Diana utterly irresistible. Madeline wondered now whether her marrying Joe had precipitated his condition. He had certainly had more responsibilities and had worked hard in the years following their wedding. But his illness had been incurable, and the doctors had told her numerous times that she had made his last years happy ones.

She decided to leave her hair loose and emerged from the bedroom looking youthfully attractive. Diana was touching up her make-up with a deft hand. She wore only dark eyeshadow and lipstick, her olive skin not requiring any further cosmetic.

She looked critically over her shoulder at her mother. 'Does Uncle Adrian approve of slacks?' she asked pointedly.

Madeline looked amused. 'I can hardly see how it matters,' she answered lightly. 'I'm wearing them, not Uncle Adrian.'

'I know, but honestly, Mum, you'll probably marry him one day and then you really will have to dress more in keeping with your position.'

'My dear Diana, I have no intention of marrying Uncle Adrian. I've told him, and incidentally you, so a hundred times. Heavens, I'm thirty-three, not fifty-three, and although I'm sure it seems a great age to you, I don't intend taking to my rocking chair yet.'

Diana frowned. 'Uncle Adrian is no older than Daddy would have been had he—' She halted.

'Oh, darling, I know. But that was different.'

'How?'

Madeline glanced at her watch. 'Isn't it time you were going?'

Her daughter shrugged. 'I suppose so. Okay, suit yourself.' She pulled on the duffel coat. 'I'll go, then.'

'All right, darling. Look after yourself.'

Diana kissed her mother's cheek and whirled out of the flat. Madeline walked into the kitchen. Evidences of Diana's hasty washing-up session were to be found on the floor which was almost swimming with water. The dish-mop was soaking and causing a wet stain to trickle over the window ledge and down the tiles to the sink.

Madeline squeezed out the dish-mop and taking the large mop she soaked up the water from the floor, wiping clean the parquet flooring. Then she put away the dishes which Diana had left on the bench, and returned to the lounge.

She had just settled herself in front of the television when the door bell pealed.

Lazily, she rose to her feet and padded to the door. Opening it, she found Adrian Sinclair waiting to be admitted.

Adrian was a tall lean man in his early fifties. Twenty years older than Madeline and a bachelor, he found his secretary utterly charming and desirable and all his hitherto undisturbed feelings were being violently churned by her apparent lack of romantic interest in him. Frankly, Madeline wondered what it was about her that appealed to older men. She found Adrian intellectually stimulating but emotionally cold, and marriages were not built on intellect alone. He made no headway in any other direction with her.

'Come in, Adrian,' she said, smiling now. 'Is it still as cold?'

'Colder,' remarked Adrian, coming in and loosening his overcoat. 'Hmm. This is a cosy room, Madeline. I always feel at home here.'

'Good. I'm pleased.' Madeline closed the door and relieved him of his coat before following him across the room. 'Do you want a drink before I sit down?'

'Thank you. I'll have a small whisky.'

Adrian seated himself on the couch in front of the television where Madeline had been seated before his arrival and after pouring the drink, Madeline joined him.

She enjoyed Adrian's companionship and his ready humour and was glad he made no strong attempts to force their relationship into anything more. He often broached the subject of marriage, but Madeline had tried to make it plain from the outset that there could never be anything more than friendship between them.

Adrian came to the flat as often as he was able, whether or not Diana was at home. He liked Diana and she was very fond of him. He had been Uncle Adrian since she was eleven years old and she saw no reason to change that now.

He owned a house in Otterbury, run for him by an efficient housekeeper. The house was near the Otterbury Secondary School of which he was headmaster, and although it was large and rather gloomy for a man living alone, he liked it, and kept it well filled with a selection of *objets d'art* which would furnish a museum. Madeline

15

had sometimes mused that should he ever marry and have children about the house he would be in an eternal state of anxiety about his collection.

'There was an accident on the Otterbury road today,' he remarked now, casually. 'Two cars and a lorry collided. It was in the late paper.'

'Oh! Was there?' Madeline suppressed her own knowledge of the accident. She had no intention of telling Adrian any more than Diana about her own mishap. Like Diana, he deplored her constant use of the scooter on the busy road and would have preferred her to use public transport on those evenings when he was unable to bring her home.

'Yes. Some people move too fast for safety. Most of these collisions could be avoided with a little forethought.'

'Oh, I agree,' averred Madeline, sitting down beside him, and hoping her face would not give her away. 'The traffic from Sheridans moves pretty fast.'

'It does indeed. I'll be glad when those houses are finished beyond the factory. Then those blighters won't have to come into Otterbury to take the London road. Most of the cars make a racetrack of that stretch outside the school. I'm eternally grateful our crowd are away before them. Can you imagine what it would be like with a swarm of cyclists leaving our gates and trying to integrate with that lot? Heaven help them!'

Madeline accepted a cigarette from him and after they were both smoking, she said: 'Have you ever been round the Sheridan factory?'

'No. Not since it was opened. I once went over the site during the early stages of construction. It's a terrific place. Apparently it will employ about five thousand men when it's fully operational. They've brought several key workers over from Italy, of course, and from their factory near Detroit. I've heard that Nicholas Vitale himself has come over from Rome to make sure everything is going satisfactorily. Of course, he's only here for a visit. He's the big boss. His father started the business, you know. A man called Masterson is running this end. He's an American, I believe, and he's bought his family over. They've leased that house near Highnook. Ingleside, I believe it's called.'

'Yes, I know the place, Adrian. It's enormous. Didn't it belong to some penniless member of the aristocracy at one time?'

'Yes. Old Lord Otterbury himself used to live there years ago.' Adrian chuckled. 'Trust Americans to install themselves in the local stately home!'

Madeline laughed. 'It must be nice to be free from money worries.'

'My dear Madeline, you too could be free from money worries if only you would let me take care of you.'

'I know, Adrian, and I appreciate it. But I just can't see myself as a headmaster's wife, dispensing tea and sympathy to the parents of the children. I'm not the type, I'm afraid.'

'Nonsense, Madeline, you would adapt yourself easily.' Adrian sighed. 'Seriously though, Diana would be agreeable to your marrying me. She's like a daughter to me already.'

'I know that, Adrian. She's a great advocate for your cause. It's simply that – well, I enjoy my freedom, and more important still – we're not in love with one another.'

'Were you in love with Joe?' Adrian frowned when Madeline did not answer. 'Besides, I do love you, Madeline. Being in love is for young people. We're adults; mature people, not teenagers hankering after the moon. Wouldn't you like to relax sometimes and put your feet up instead of rushing out to school every morning and working all day just to rush home again in the evenings?'

Madeline sighed. All that Adrian had said was true. Diana would be delighted if they got married. Indeed she would be very enthusiastic. She liked and respected Adrian and would enjoy the social distinction of being the headmaster's stepdaughter. And Madeline knew how pleasant it would be to have loads of spare time to read all the books she would like to read; explore all the museums and art galleries that she enjoyed visiting; maybe even have a larger family.

At this she drew herself up with a start. She could never resign herself again to a life like that. She was not a mercenary person at heart and the idea of marrying someone for the material benefits that were to be enjoyed appalled her. She couldn't do it. She and Diana had managed alone this far, and in a couple of years Diana would be working and able to supply herself with the little luxuries that Madeline could not always afford.

'I'm sorry, Adrian,' she said, sighing again. 'I couldn't do it. Much as I like and respect you, I don't see how we could make a go of it. You're too set in your ways to change anyway. You would hate having a teenager in the house, upsetting your precious collection and rousing you at all hours to the sound of the latest pop group. You have no idea what it would be like.'

'Nonsense,' said Adrian once more. Then he sighed as he saw the reluctance on her face. 'All right. Forget it. Anyway, where is Diana tonight?'

'She's gone to the Seventies Club with Jeffrey Emerson. Do you know him?'

'I know of him,' replied Adrian thoughtfully. 'His brother is in the first year at my school, but Jeffrey goes to the Grammar, doesn't he?'

'Yes. He's only seventeen. He has taken his Advanced Levels in G.C.E. and now he's waiting for a place at university.'

'Ah, yes. I remember Hetherington was talking about him the last time we had dinner together.' Mr. Hetherington was the headmaster of the Grammar School. 'He said that his mother is quite different, however. He can hardly believe that Jeffrey is her son. She's quite coarse, I believe.'

Madeline bit her lip. 'Jeffrey is quite a handsome boy and as you say he is intelligent, but I wonder sometimes if he's a little wild, at least away from school.'

Adrian frowned. 'Yes. Maybe.' He looked ponderous. 'Are you worried about his influence on Diana?'

'Yes. Yes, I am.'

'But Diana isn't a tearaway.'

'Oh, I know.' Madeline moved restlessly. 'It's just that she's so young.'

Adrian shrugged. 'They mature earlier these days. Diana is a sensible girl. She would never behave stupidly.'

'Wouldn't she?' Madeline rose to her feet. 'Wouldn't she?' She smiled. 'No. I suppose not.'

Adrian smiled too. 'Look, I know how you feel. You're her guardian. You feel doubly responsible because she has no father.'

'What . . . what does Jeffrey's father do?'

'He works for a firm of haulage contractors,' answered Adrian. 'As I said before, Jeffrey is certainly the changeling in that family.'

The Seventies Club was located over a coffee bar of the same name in Otterbury High Street. Its members were all teenagers from the local schools or the technical colleges and the music was provided by a jukebox which was provided free by the owner.

This Friday evening it was packed with youngsters, all gyrating and turning madly to the lusty music issuing from the jukebox. A low bar along one wall served coffee or Coca-Cola and the lighting was subdued and mellow.

Diana Scott and Jeffrey Emerson were dancing together and as the music ended, Diana collapsed, laughing, against her partner.

'Gosh,' she exclaimed, 'I'm fagged out. Shall we sit down for a while?'

Jeffrey grinned down at her, and his arms closed round her, holding her a prisoner.

'I'd rather stay like this,' he murmured softly, and Diana blushed scarlet. She liked Jeff very much and was pleased that lately their relationship seemed to be entering a more serious stage. She had never had a steady boy-friend before and she wanted to be like the other girls who spent their time discussing the merits of different boys.

She wriggled free, however, and holding his hand, she drew him across the room to the bar. They perched on stools together and Jeffrey ordered two coffees and took out a packet of cigarettes which he offered to Diana. Diana shook her head and Jeffrey lit his own and put them back in his pocket.

'I thought you intended to try smoking sometimes,' he remarked lazily.

'I did . . . I do.' Diana bit her lip.

'You're frightened,' he jeered, and she stiffened her shoulders.

'No, I'm not. Give me one.'

Shrugging, Jeff handed her a cigarette and lit it. Diana drew on it as she had seen other people doing and then began to cough chokingly.

Jeff grinned and pounded her on the back and Diana shuddered.

'Ugh, it's horrible!' she exclaimed. 'I don't know how you can.'

'You must persevere,' said Jeff. 'Go on, have another drag.'

'No, thank you.' Diana was adamant. She threw the cigarette on the floor and put her foot on it.

'Hey!' Jeff was indignant. 'They don't grow on trees, you know.'

'No. Plants,' replied Diana sarcastically, and Jeff looked furious.

'Very amusing,' he said coldly, and stalked off across the dance floor.

Diana was flabbergasted. She had never dreamed he would walk away and leave her. Her heart was pounding rapidly and she felt herself going cold inside.

She knew that all the other girls at the Club envied her her association with Jeffrey Emerson. He was a very at-tractive boy and could have his pick of the girls. That he should choose her had always thrilled her enormously because prior to the last two months he had treated her like a child. Since she had started at the Commercial College she had grown up greatly and did not realize just how appealing she was with her silky hair and wide eyes. When he had started dating her, her prestige with the others had gone up a lot, and part of his attraction was that he was the current heart-throb.

The music had started again and she saw him approach a slim, fair girl and obviously ask her to dance. Diana felt hurt and angry. How dared he treat her like this? She had a good mind to go home. But she knew she wouldn't. She would wait and see whether he came back. It was galling, but she couldn't walk out on him. Not now.

She ordered another coffee and sat sipping it pensively. If he didn't come back between dances she would have to go home. It would be awful!

She was in the depths of despair, two dances later, when she was aware that someone had joined her. Hardly daring to look round, she gave him a sidelong glance. To her relief, it was Jeff.

Jeff's face was rather remote, but he said:

'Do you want to dance?'

Diana felt her hands go clammy. 'I . . . well, do you?'

He shrugged. 'Yes. I'm going to dance,' he replied coolly.

'All right.' She slid off her stool.

The music was slow and haunting now, a love-song being crooned by a current disc idol. Jeff drew her into his arms and put his cheek against her hair. They moved slowly, their arms wrapped round each other. Diana could feel herself trembling and he murmured: 'Relax.'

'I'm sorry,' she whispered, aware of herself apologizing for nothing. But anything was better than his indifference.

Jeff looked down at her. 'Are you?' he asked.

'Why did you walk away?' she murmured, looking anxious.

'I don't like being treated like an idiot.'

'But I wasn't ... oh, Jeff, I guess I am silly at times. Can't we forget about it?'

Jeff's eyes softened. 'All right, Diana. I guess I was as much to blame for taking the huff. Did I make you jealous?'

Diana blushed. 'Yes, you succeeded in that direction,' she remarked softly, against his neck, and felt his arms tighten possessively about her.

When the music ended he glanced at his watch.

'It's nine-thirty,' he said quietly. 'Let's go, hmn?'

She nodded and went to collect her coat. Outside the air was clear but bitterly cold and they walked swiftly along to the bus stop. Jeff lived at the opposite end of Otterbury, near the secondary school, in fact, but he always saw Diana right home.

The bus dropped them at the end of Evenwood Gardens and they walked up the darkened road towards the second block of flats where the Scotts lived. Before they reached the second block, between the two tall buildings, was a small ornamental garden with flower beds and a bench set among rose trees and rhododendron bushes. The last few dates they had had together had ended on the bench where they said a prolonged goodnight to each other. Although it was cold they still walked through the gardens to the bench, but they did not sit down tonight. It had been raining earlier in the day and everywhere was still slightly damp, but the bushes at least provided a little privacy.

'Well,' said Diana, looking up at Jeff, 'thanks for bringing me home.'

'It was a pleasure,' he said softly, pulling her to him, close against his warm body. 'Oh, Diana,' he groaned urgently, and his mouth met hers.

Diana slid her arms around him, returning his kiss more responsively than ever. Their minor upset this evening had merely served as an incentive to their mutual attraction for one another and Diana, no less than Jeff, found something infinitely more absorbing in their embrace than ever before.

Diana knew very little about kissing of this kind, not being as old as Jeff or as experienced, but she was aware of a kind of danger not far away. Something about his intense hold on her and the increased tenor of his breathing warned her he was emotionally disturbed in a way hitherto unknown to her. With a feeling of revulsion, she suddenly drew back and swallowed hard.

Jeff fastened his overcoat with unsteady fingers and said:

'Have you any idea what kissing like that does to a fellow?' in a tight, withdrawn voice.

Diana bit her lip and clenched her fists. 'Is . . . is something wrong?' she asked nervously.

Jeff laughed shortly and mirthlessly. 'Oh, no. Not at all.' He looked furious. 'Look, I've got to go.'

'Will . . . will I see you tomorrow?'

Jeff hesitated, and then hunched his shoulders. 'Oh, yes, I guess so. I have a lecture in the morning, but tomorrow afternoon I'm refereeing the rugby match. Would you like to come?'

'Could I?' Diana was interested.

'Of course. We could have tea afterwards at my mother's and then go to the pictures in the evening. If you'd like to.'

Diana looked more at ease. 'I'd love to, you know that. Will your mother mind?'

Jeff shook his head. 'Of course not. Well?'

Diana smiled. 'All right.'

Jeff managed a smile in return and thrust his hands into the pockets of his coat. 'I must go now,' he said. 'See you tomorrow. We'll meet at the school.'

He left her at the entrance to the flats and then walked back down the gardens to catch his bus.

When Diana opened the door of the flat and went in she found her mother just preparing coffee and sandwiches in the kitchen while Adrian Sinclair was stretched out on the settee watching the television. It was apparently the repeat of a football match held in some continental country and after greeting Diana, Adrian returned to his viewing while Diana went out to the kitchen to see her mother.

Madeline smiled cheerfully at her. 'Well?' she said. 'Did you have a good time?'

'Yes, thanks,' said Diana, sighing a little as she remembered the kiss they had exchanged. She supposed idly it was the first real kiss she had ever experienced. Prior to tonight all the kisses she had been given were light, casual affairs, and even Jeff had been the same. Now suddenly it was all different. Tonight's kiss had been full of emotions that she had not realized existed.

Madeline was looking at her curiously and she asked: 'Why the faraway look in your eyes? Where have you been?'

'Just to the Club,' exclaimed Diana, flushing and feeling rather embarrassed. 'I . . . we . . . I'll go and get undressed, Mum, and then I can go straight to bed after supper.'

'All right, darling.' Madeline frowned to herself. There was something different about Diana tonight and she couldn't decide what it was. It disturbed her to realize that Diana was getting to the stage where she did not tell her mother everything.

CHAPTER TWO

On Saturday morning, Madeline and Diana usually went shopping together. They bought most of the food required for the following week and the perishable goods were stored in the pocket-sized refrigerator, in the kitchen.

'I'm going to the grammar school rugby match with Jeff this afternoon,' remarked Diana, as they ate their lunch. 'Then we're going to have tea at his home and go on to the pictures.'

'Really?' Madeline raised her dark eyebrows. 'Will his mother be pleased about that?'

Diana smiled. 'Why shouldn't she be? Besides, we won't be there long.'

'Have you met his family before?'

'No. But that doesn't matter.'

Madeline shrugged. 'Well, I hope everything turns out all right. Does this portend a more serious relationship in the future? I hope not. You're very young, both of you.'

'Oh, Mother!' Diana exclaimed, and carried her dessert plate through to the kitchen.

While she was making the coffee her mother joined her, her expression thoughtful.

'Just remember,' went on Madeline quietly, 'you're still only a child and Jeff is still at school. He intends to go to university in the autumn, so you've told me, so it's no use either of you doing anything silly.'

'I don't see that you've any reason to talk to me like this,' protested Diana exasperatedly. She hated being talked down to. 'After all, I've not said anything, have I?'

'No. But last night you looked rather strange, when you came home.'

Diana felt her cheeks flame again. It was annoying to

be so transparent.

'For no reason,' she retorted abruptly, and turned off the percolator.

Madeline wondered, was she being over-anxious about Diana? After all, as Adrian said, girls did mature earlier these days. She hoped so; how she hoped so!

After the meal was over Madeline washed up while Diana went to change. Then she got out the vacuum cleaner. She always did the apartment through on Saturday afternoons.

Diana emerged looking young and fresh in a tweed skirt and a chunky sweater. She was wearing a quilted anorak with a hood which actually belonged to Madeline and which was the colour of honey with a darker brown lining. It suited Diana's olive colouring as much as Madeline's and she looked rather ruefully at her mother.

'You don't mind, do you?' she asked, indicating the anorak.

Madeline grimaced, an amused look on her face, 'Would it matter if I did?' she asked, smiling. 'No, go on. It will at least keep you warm. And you're wearing your new boots, I see. I'm glad you got them, even if they were expensive.'

'Well,' said Diana, 'I want to look nice to meet his parents.'

'Y . . . yes,' said Madeline doubtfully. 'Oh, well . . .' she shrugged. 'Have fun!'

'I will. G'bye.'

After Diana had gone, Madeline set to work with a vengeance. She was not particularly fond of housework, but it had to be done and she was not one for shirking it.

By the time she had finished it was teatime, so she made herself a snack. Adrian always took her out for dinner on Saturday evenings, so she did not bother with much of a meal. They usually went to a hotel just outside Otterbury, and had a drink before the meal. Madeline always enjoyed the change it made as she did not go out at all during the week.

She changed into a jersey dress of amber-coloured material and combed her hair up into the French knot. As she applied a light make-up to her face she thought that at least her skin was good. It was smooth and unlined and she was aware that she did look younger than her thirty-three years. Amused at her thoughts, she realized that all this self-criticism had been brought on by the man in the red car and she wondered again whether she would see him any more.

Adrian arrived at seven-thirty. Dressed in a fawn lounge suit he, too, looked younger and distinguished, and Madeline smiled as she admitted him.

'You look very smart this evening,' she complimented him.

Adrian raised his eyebrows. 'Thank you. So do you. The Crown won't really do us justice, will it?'

Madeline pulled on a loose suede coat. 'I expect it will be as pleasant as usual,' she replied, matter-of-factly.

Adrian drove an old Rover which was remarkably comfortable. He was always saying he would have to get a new one, but Madeline knew his old car would survive a few more years yet. Adrian disliked change. He was a creature of habit. That was why she knew that she could never think seriously of marriage with him, if for no other reason than his staid ways.

The Crown was only three miles from Otterbury, on the Guildford road. It was a reasonably sized hotel, catering mainly for evening motorists who wanted to get away from the noise and bustle of the towns. It had built up a reputation for good service over the years and its restaurant was both efficient and well patronized. The food, cooked by a French chef, was delicious and varied in taste and Madeline always felt quite a gourmet eating there.

The road to the Crown ran past the Sheridan factory, and she felt her eyes drawn to the place as they passed. She wondered what position the man held. He had said he worked at Sheridans, so he was possibly one of the managers. Driving the kind of automobile he drove, she hardly associated him with the shop floor. Besides, his

27

clothes had had that definite air of good tailoring about them, and even Adrian's suits did not fit him so well or look so expensive as that. And Adrian was a headmaster! But then Adrian bought things to last and they usually did.

The Crown was very crowded, but their table was reserved week by week, so that at least was secure. Since the arrival of the Italians and Americans the town of Otterbury and its environs seemed to be getting smaller and the population was overrunning its limits everywhere. Adrian grumbled as he had to push his way through to the bar for their drinks. He fought his way back to her side as she stood near the entrance. He was carrying a vodka for her and a whisky for himself.

'What a scrum!' he muttered, easing himself into a position beside her. 'It's getting more like a rugby match every week. It never used to be like this.'

'I don't suppose the proprietors are grumbling,' remarked Madeline wryly. 'They'll be grateful for the trade.'

'I expect they are, but really, there's nowhere to sit, and the fumes over by the bar are nauseating.'

Madeline smiled. She was not as averse to crowds as Adrian, but even she could see that there was not much fun in standing in the doorway all evening.

'Let's go and have our supper then,' she said. 'After all, we can have a drink in there in comparative luxury.'

'An excellent idea,' said Adrian at once. 'Lead on.'

The supper room, too, was crowded, but Adrian's table, under the window was waiting for them. They seated themselves thankfully, and Madeline removed her coat.

They ate grilled salmon and peach soufflé, and Madeline sighed with enjoyment as she sipped her coffee.

'That was absolutely delicious,' she murmured, smiling. 'You must admit, Adrian, if we were to change our hotel, we wouldn't get a meal like that.'

Adrian smiled. 'Yes, you're probably right. I feel altogether different about things now.'

They lit cigarettes and were idly discussing a novel they had both read when a shadow fell across the table. Madeline looked up in surprise to see an elderly man smiling down on them. Adrian, looking up too, rose swiftly to his feet.

'Hetherington!' he exclaimed. 'It's a long while since we've met.'

Mr. Hetherington smiled benignly down and said:

'May I join you for a moment?'

'Of course, sit down,' said Adrian easily. 'Oh, by the way, this is my secretary, Mrs. Scott. I don't believe you've met before. Madeline, this is Mr. Hetherington, the headmaster of the Grammar School.'

'Yes, I know,' said Madeline, smiling, and shaking hands with Mr. Hetherington. 'Do sit down. We have finished.'

Hetherington seated himself in the vacant chair and said:

'I see you like the cuisine here, too.'

'Oh, yes,' said Madeline enthusiastically. 'Do you come here often?'

'Only as often as I can safely leave my wife,' replied Hetherington slowly. 'She's a semi-invalid, you know, and I don't like leaving her alone. However, I had a business engagement this evening and we came on here for a meal, afterwards.' He turned to Adrian. 'I'm glad I've run into you, Sinclair. I wanted a word with you.'

'Oh, yes?' Adrian was intrigued. 'What about?'

'Shall I leave you?' Madeline looked questioningly at Hetherington.

Hetherington shook his head and taking out his pipe he began to fill it.

'Not at all,' he replied. 'Do you mind if I smoke?'

Madeline said: 'No, not at all,' and Hetherington lit his pipe ponderously.

'Now,' he said, when he had it going, 'you know Conrad Masterson, don't you, Sinclair?'

Adrian frowned. 'Conrad Masterson? No. Who's he? Oh, wait a minute, you don't mean the American who's now running the Sheridan factory?'

'That's right. Do you know him?'

Adrian shook his head. 'No. I've only heard his name in passing. Why?'

'Well, you'll know he's bought that house that used to belong to Lord Otterbury at Highnook.'

'Yes, I had heard,' Adrian nodded, and Madeline listened interestedly. What was all this about?

'Well, I have his son, Conrad junior, at school. He's thirteen and quite a bright boy. But that's not what I was going to tell you.' He chuckled. He was quite aware that his colleague was positively bursting with curiosity for him to get to the point. 'No, actually, Masterson himself came in to see me earlier in the week and invited me and my wife to go up to his house for a drink on Monday evening. I explained that Mary was not up to social visiting, so he suggested that I came anyway and brought along anyone I cared to. I wondered whether you might like to come along with me. Like most Americans, Masterson is very gregarious and he wants to get to know people. Naturally, your position as headmaster of the only other secondary school in the town brought your name first to my mind. I was going to ring you tomorrow, but when I saw you here this evening, I couldn't miss the opportunity to speak to you myself. I hope you don't think I'm intruding?'

'Not at all.' Adrian was obviously intrigued and flattered. 'It sounds a most fascinating prospect. I must admit these newcomers to our town interest me enormously.'

Madeline hid a smile as she remembered his antipathy earlier in the evening when he had had to struggle to get drinks simply because of the crowd of newcomers.

'I've never visited America,' Adrian went on, 'and I should welcome the chance to discuss the country with people who really know what they're talking about. Of course I'll come.'

'Good. Good,' Hetherington smiled in satisfaction. 'I too think it should prove quite a stimulating affair.' He turned to Madeline. 'Do you enjoy working for our distinguished friend, Mrs. Scott?'

Madeline smiled. 'Very much, thank you. Adrian is a very considerate employer; not a slave-driver.'

Hetherington puffed at his pipe. 'Yes, I should think he would be, with a pretty thing like you. Can't you jolt him out of his bachelor state? I understand you're a widow.'

Madeline looked down at her cigarette and then with a twinkle in her eyes, she said: 'I think Adrian is quite happy as he is, don't you?' She controlled her laughter.

'We're not children,' remarked Adrian sarcastically, not at all amused. In his opinion, Hetherington was too keen on making preposterous remarks and getting away with them.

'No, I'm sure you're not,' agreed Hetherington, chuckling himself. 'Anyway, Sinclair, why don't you ask Mrs. Scott if she would care to accompany us on Monday evening? I think she would enjoy it, too.'

'I'm sure she would,' said Adrian, nodding his approval. 'Will you come, Madeline?'

'I ... I don't know,' she began awkwardly. 'I wasn't invited, and I really don't think....'

'Nonsense,' exclaimed Hetherington, shaking his head. 'Masterson will be only too delighted to welcome you. And after all, you won't be alone. Adrian will be there beside you.'

Madeline hesitated, and Adrian urged her to accept. 'Please say you'll come, Madeline,' he coaxed her, persuasively.

'But Diana—'

'—is quite capable of taking care of herself for one evening,' said Adrian firmly. 'Yes, Hetherington, we'll both come. Shall I pick you up?'

'Well ... yes. That would be best, and then you can collect Mrs. Scott.' He rose to his feet. 'And now I must go and allow you to continue your evening uninterrupted.' His eyes twinkled. 'Keep him in order, Mrs. Scott.'

Madeline laughed at Adrian's outraged countenance and Hetherington walked away, still chuckling.

'Really!' exclaimed Adrian exasperatedly. 'He really is the limit! Who does he think he is?'

'He's a rather charming old man,' remarked Madeline mildly. 'I like him. He was only joking. Adrian, don't get so heated over nothing.'

Adrian sighed and smiled ruefully. 'I suppose you're right as usual. He always makes me feel like one of his pupils, I'm afraid.'

Madeline laughed merrily. 'Rather an old pupil, wouldn't you say?' she said cheerfully.

After they left the Crown they drove back to Madeline's flat. It was only about ten o'clock, so she invited Adrian in for more coffee. Diana was not in when they arrived, but she came in soon after.

She was flushed and not as full of daydreams as the previous evening and Madeline felt rather relieved, if a trifle apprehensive about her rather dejected expression. She had not known how to deal with her the previous evening and it was obvious that she did not know how to deal with her tonight either. She decided to play the game as it was played to her and refused to start worrying again after such a pleasant and relaxing evening.

'Have you had a nice evening?' Diana asked, looking across at Adrian.

Adrian sank down into the comfort of the couch. 'Very nice, thank you, Diana. Come and tell me about that boyfriend of yours. Did he give you a good time?'

'Yes, thank you,' said Diana politely. She pulled off the anorak and sat down beside him. 'We had tea at his mother's and then we went to the pictures. We saw a Western epic at the Odeon.'

'I see. Was it good?'

Diana wrinkled her nose. 'It was all right,' she conceded. 'We don't always see a lot of the film,' she remarked, watching idly for Adrian's shocked expression.

She was not disappointed. Adrian raised his eyebrows in disapproval. Her outspoken words had shocked him. She was certainly changing this elf-like daughter of Madeline's. Madeline was right. She was becoming a handful.

'How was the tea?' asked Madeline herself, coming through from the kitchen, with a tray of coffee. 'Did you get on all right with his parents?'

Diana shrugged her slim shoulders eloquently. 'I suppose so. His mother made some rather barbed comments about Jeff neglecting his studies recently, as though I was the entire cause, and that he would have to pick himself up if he was expecting them to send him to university in the autumn. Poor Jeff!' Diana sighed in remembrance. 'He looked positively furious and told her rather rudely that it was his affair whether or not he went to the university. I think he's having second thoughts.'

'I see.' Madeline ran a tongue over her lips. 'But of course, you told him he must go to the university, didn't you, Diana? He's quite a clever boy. His headmaster says so. You mustn't come between him and his work.'

Diana looked mutinous, but remained silent, and Adrian and Madeline exchanged glances.

'What did you have for supper?' asked Diana suddenly, changing the subject, and shrugging, Madeline related the events of their evening, describing their meeting with Hetherington and his subsequent invitation to visit the Mastersons.

'Gosh!' Diana sounded envious. 'Do you think I could come?'

Adrian frowned. 'I'm afraid not, Diana. This is a grown-up affair. It would probably bore you to tears.'

Diana compressed her lips. 'Grown-up,' she muttered. 'What am I?'

Adrian reached for his cigarette case. 'Little more than a schoolgirl,' he replied smoothly. 'Diana, you have years and years ahead of you. Enjoy what's yours today. Don't hanker over the future before it arrives.'

Diana sighed. 'Uncle Adrian, I don't want a lecture. Anyway, I think it will be jolly exciting. Who will be there?'

'Oh, the executives from the factory, I expect,' replied Adrian. 'They're mostly married men, with their families over here. As I've said, it's a pretty dull affair.'

'What on earth shall I wear?' exclaimed Madeline suddenly.

'You'll think of something,' replied Adrian, smiling. 'I'd better give old Hetherington a ring tomorrow and find out what time we have to be there. I should hate us to arrive while they're having dinner.'

'Oh, yes,' nodded Madeline. 'You can let me know on Monday.' She stretched lazily. 'I'm tired. It's been a long day.'

'That's my cue,' murmured Adrian dryly, rising to his feet. 'I'll be off. Will I see you tomorrow?'

'You can come round if you want to,' said Madeline easily. 'Please yourself. If not I'll see you Monday morning.'

'Right. Good night, then. Good night, Diana.'

'Good night, Uncle Adrian,' said Diana, kissing his cheek. 'Mind how you go.'

After Adrian had gone, Madeline carried the dishes into the kitchen and Diana followed her and picked up the tea towel to dry them.

'Are you seeing Jeff tomorrow?' asked Madeline, turning on the hot tap.

'Yes. Why? Do you want me for something?' Diana frowned.

'Oh ... er ... no.' Madeline smiled rather uncertainly at her daughter. 'Where are you going then?'

'Well, actually, just for a walk in the afternoon,' replied Diana quietly.

'Would you like to bring him back here for tea?'

Diana's eyes brightened. 'Could I?' Jeff had only been to tea once before at the flat and then Madeline had had a headache and had had to leave them to their own devices.

She smiled now. 'Of course. After tea, if Uncle Adrian comes round, we might play Monopoly or something.'

Diana looked disgusted. 'Oh, Mum, Jeff and I won't want to play games!'

Madeline shrugged. 'All right. What will you do then?'

'We might go to the Seventies Club.'

Madeline frowned. She did not like the idea of Diana going to a place like that on a Sunday evening, but alternatively it was better to know they were there, rather than wandering round the streets.

'All right,' she said, 'you do what you like.'

CHAPTER THREE

DURING Monday, Madeline found her thoughts straying often to the evening ahead. It was quite an occasion for her to go out during the week. Now and then she and Adrian would take the train to London and go and see a show or listen to a concert at the Royal Festival Hall, but these outings were few and far between as Adrian was usually busy during the week, and besides, there was Diana to consider. She was still very young to be left too long alone and Madeline always put her first.

On Sunday Adrian had come to high tea at the flat and met Jeff. They had had quite a good time together. Jeff was intelligent and could discuss topics with Adrian which neither of the women could have done. Madeline found him quite charming and wondered whether she was worrying unduly about Diana. After all, surely young people could be friendly without getting themselves into bother. He was a nice-looking boy and whatever his background he was able to take care of himself and act as politely as the next person.

At lunchtime on Monday, Madeline went into the town centre. She had decided to treat herself to a new dress for the evening. She rarely indulged herself, except for necessities, and even Diana had gone as far as to say that this kind of affair did not happen every day. Madeline suspected that Diana was hoping for some development in her relationship with Adrian, and if so, Madeline knew she was going to be disappointed.

She found what she wanted in a small dress shop in Gilesgate. It was more than she had expected to pay, but she couldn't resist it after trying it on. It was a delicious shade of leaf green chiffon, an ankle-length dress with sequins studded on the bodice. The neckline was low and round and embroidered with tiny beads and it had long sleeves which ended in cuffs, also embroidered with beads. It was the ideal dress for the occasion and she took it back to work feeling very pleased with her expedition. When Adrian asked to see it later in the afternoon she refused to show it to him.

'Wait until tonight,' she said teasingly. 'I want to surprise you.'

Adrian chuckled. 'All right, my dear, have it your own way. But I shall expect you to model it before we leave for the party.'

Madeline smiled and shook her head. Really, Adrian was a dear, she thought, sighing. Why couldn't she decide to marry him and be done with it?

They were due at the Mastersons' at nine o'clock and Adrian called at ten minutes to nine. He had already collected Mr. Hetherington and he was waiting in the car when they went down. Diana was not going out this evening. Jeff was studying and she had decided to wash her hair and play her records.

Madeline was wearing a brushed wool coat in a creamy colour and for once had left her hair loose on her shoulders. She looked about twenty-five and Diana had said, rather scathingly:

'Good heavens, Mum, no one will believe you have a daughter of over sixteen!'

'That's all to the good, surely?' Madeline had answered, but Diana had sounded non-committal. Madeline wondered whether the fact of Diana losing Joe at such an early age had made her doubly dependent on herself, and doubly willing to resent her mother's youthful appearance. It was as though she was afraid Madeline might forget she had a daughter altogether, which was ridiculous.

Of course, Joe had been so much older, and Diana would have obviously greatly preferred a homely, buxom type without any pretensions to attraction. Perhaps her campaign on Adrian's behalf was fixed on the idea that as Adrian was middle-aged he might tone her mother down somewhat.

Madeline was amused at her speculations. Ought she

indeed to make Adrian and Diana happy and marry him after all? But then she squashed the idea. It wouldn't make anybody happy really. The novelty of having a headmaster as her stepfather would wear off with Diana if he tried to press any restriction upon her; Adrian would be continually in a state about his precious collection and Madeline – well! she would be utterly bored by the whole affair. Nothing, not even security, was worth that much.

Hetherington was most complimentary about her appearance. Adrian had already said how delightful she looked in the new dress, so Madeline felt sure she was going to enjoy herself, and relaxed completely.

The Mastersons' house, Ingleside, was not far away. Standing in its own grounds and floodlit by night, it looked very impressive as they turned between the permanently open drive gates. There were several cars parked in front of the house on the gravelled courtyard. Madeline saw that most of them were the wide, luxurious type, made by the Sheridan factory and its counterparts. They looked superlatively comfortable and she envied their occupants such vehicular superiority. There were several Sheridans like the one into which she had skidded last week on her scooter, but not one red one.

The house, which had been built during the sixteenth century, had been renovated extensively and although from the outside it looked typically Elizabethan, inside central heating, electric lights and fitted carpets had done away with much of its atmosphere.

The hall, wide and high with a carved roof was lit by electric candelabra, set at intervals round the walls giving a restful, luminous quality to the polished panelling and oak furniture. The floor, too had been polished and was ideal for dancing. However, most of the guests seemed to have congregated in a large lounge to the right of the hall and the manservant who had admitted them and taken their coats went into the lounge to advise his employers of their arrival.

Madeline was entranced by the place and was fascinatedly studying the minstrels' gallery when a dainty little woman in rich purple pants and blouse came out of the lounge to greet them. She introduced herself as Lucie Masterson, and said that her husband would join them later.

'He's closeted with Nicholas – you know, Nicholas Vitale, at the moment,' she said, after she had discovered their identity. 'They're always talking business these days. I do hope you won't think he's being rude. But Nicholas is the boss and they do have a lot to discuss while he's here.'

'That's quite all right, Mrs. Masterson,' replied Hetherington, smiling. 'We understand.'

'Good,' Lucie beamed. She could have been any age between thirty-five and forty-five, speculated Madeline, who thought she seemed a rather shallow woman at first appraisal.

Lucie drew them into the throng in the lounge. There were about thirty guests, all standing around drinking cocktails and exchanging small talk. A radiogram played soft music in a corner and there was an aroma of French perfume and Havana tobacco. A rich red carpet covered the floor, the colour of which was echoed in the heavy velvet curtains. There were couches and armchairs upholstered in soft leather while the white walls were relieved of starkness by vivid prints.

Many of the guests seemed to be married couples, Madeline discovered, as Lucie introduced them around. There was an almost equal number of Italians and Americans, and Lucie explained that Sheridans had factories in both countries as well as here. When Adrian and Mr. Hetherington got caught up in technical discussions with some of the older guests present Madeline found herself beside a young American couple called Fran and Dave Madison.

'Do you live in Otterbury,' asked Fran, interestedly, as Madeline accepted a cigarette from Dave.

'Yes. I have a flat not far from here, actually,' replied Madeline. 'Do you?'

'Yes. We, too, have a flat,' confirmed Dave. 'But we're expecting to have a house soon in the new development near the factory later in the year.'

'Oh, I see. You're from America?'

'That's right,' Dave grinned. 'I guess the accent is unmistakable.'

Madeline chuckled. 'I thought you might have been here visiting the Mastersons,' she said. She looked at Fran. 'Do you like England?'

'It's okay, I guess,' said Fran, without enthusiasm. 'There's not much to do, is there? We're hoping to go to Italy later on. Have you ever been abroad?'

'Just to France,' said Madeline ruefully. 'Since my husband died, my daughter and I don't go away a lot.'

'You have a daughter?' exclaimed Dave in surprise. 'A baby daughter?'

'No. Actually, she's sixteen,' replied Madeline, smiling. 'But thank you for those few kind words.'

'They weren't kind,' exclaimed Dave, grinning. 'I wouldn't say you looked more than twenty-five or six.'

Fran was looking a little put out now and Madeline was glad when another man came to join them. He was like Dave, tall and fair, with pleasant freckly features.

'Hi there, you two,' he said easily, obviously knowing the Madisons well. 'Have we got a new member of the organization?'

'No,' answered Dave, turning to him. 'Madeline, this is Harvey Cummings – he, too, is a member of the Sheridan clan.'

'How do you do,' said Madeline politely, nodding at the newcomer.

'I'm fine,' answered Harvey, grinning. 'Especially when a lovely woman is interested. Say, do you have a husband somewhere around?'

'I'm a widow,' replied Madeline, her cheeks reddening. His rather direct approach was a little disconcerting, to say the last.

'Great. I mean great for me,' said Harvey exuberantly. 'I thought you looked rather lonely and unattached. May

I attach myself to you?'

Madeline looked rather helplessly at the Madisons. 'Is your wife not here?' she asked cautiously.

Dave roared with laughter. 'Harvey married? Are you kidding? Who would take on a liability like him?'

'Take no notice,' said Harvey with mock disdain. 'It's simply that no one understands me.'

Madeline laughed. She was enjoying this good-natured bantering. It was so long since she had been in company young enough to indulge in it. Adrian, although easygoing in his own way, was definitely not the type to make fun of himself. And even Joe had had no time for facetiousness, and because of her early marriage Madeline had missed out on this kind of lighthearted interchange.

'Oh, here's Con,' said Dave suddenly. 'And our illustrious chief. They must have finished their business.'

Madeline and the others looked round. Two men were entering the room, both tall, but one was broader in the shoulders with lean good looks. They were both dressed in dark suits, but the broad-shouldered man was much darker skinned than his companion and was immediately recognizable to Madeline as the man who had driven the red car. Who was he? Conrad Masterson or Nicholas Vitale? Surely it could not be the latter!

'Which one is Mr. Masterson?' she asked Fran softly.

'Why, the one on the left, honey,' replied Fran. 'Don't you know him?'

'No, I'm afraid not. So the darker man is Nicholas Vitale?'

'Yes — handsome, isn't he? He's Italian, of course. That's why he's so dark-skinned. He's spent a lot of time in the States. We all fell for him, naturally. But as you can see, I settled for Dave.' She laughed at Dave's indignant face. 'Darling, Nicholas is the most elusive male since Adam!'

Madeline felt her stomach turn over. She had skidded into the car belonging to the owner of Sheridans. No wonder he had been annoyed!

Nicholas Vitale surveyed the throng in the lounge of the Mastersons' house with cynical boredom in his eyes. Gatherings of this nature always bored him. Too much to drink and too many predatory females hanging around him. Had he not had business with Conrad Masterson he would not have been here tonight. He had found a small club in London which was much more to his taste. However, he was here now, and he was expected to stay at least for an interval.

His keen eyes searched the room for Harvey Cummings. Harvey was his personal assistant and public relations man. Harvey liked these kind of affairs and in truth they had had some good times together, but somehow he didn't feel he was going to enjoy himself tonight.

He saw Harvey almost at once. He was standing with Dave Madison and his wife and another girl. He supposed the girl must be with Harvey.

Excusing himself from his host, he made his way through the chattering crowds to Harvey's side. He acknowledged the greetings of the other guests in passing, but to the regret of the female contingency, he did not stop to talk. Everyone knew who he was, of course, and he knew they would be speculating about his activities. His private life was practically non-existent at times and he knew he had a ruthless reputation where women were concerned. To a certain extent his reputation was justified, but Nicholas himself was well aware that the women who involved themselves in his life expected no more than he gave them. If they were willing to play the game Nicholas's way, he was certainly not the man to complain. Only Harvey of his circle of associates ever saw the real man behind the mask of diplomacy.

Harvey and his girl-friend were absorbed in conversation as he approached them and he had time to wonder who the girl was and what they were talking about. She was tall and slim and had hair of a very unusual and lovely colour. It swung loosely on her shoulders and looked thick and silky. He mused that Harvey could

42

usually pick his women.

Putting a hand on Harvey's shoulder, he said:

'Do you mind if I break up this tête-à-tête?'

Harvey swung round and groaned. 'God, I thought it was the law! Must you creep up on a guy like that?'

Nicholas grinned, and then his eyes narrowed. The girl with Harvey was known to him. She had been riding the scooter which had bumped into his car last Friday. She had obviously recognized him, too, for her face was suddenly suffused with colour.

'Well, well,' he drawled. 'The world is really a small place.'

Harvey looked puzzled. 'How's that? Do you two know one another?'

'Mrs. ... er ... Scott and I collided last Friday,' said Nicholas dryly. 'I was in my car at the time and she was riding a scooter.'

'Indeed?' Harvey raised his eyebrows. 'Say, Madeline, you didn't say you knew Nick when he walked in.'

'I don't ... that is. ...' Madeline felt schoolgirlishly embarrassed. 'Mr. Vitale merely helped me up, that's all. We were hardly introduced.'

Nicholas was amused. Last week he had thought she had a very interesting face, but tonight she was quite lovely. He wanted to know more about her. He had taken down the number of her scooter as she was riding away and he had intended finding out more about her. What was she doing with Harvey? Particularly if she was married? He had no scruples about the kind of married women he knew, who invariably were involved with some man or other, but this creature was different. She wasn't like the usual run of his acquaintances. She had a clear, open countenance; honest, you might say, and beautiful, wide eyes.

'Be a pal, and get me a drink, Harvey,' he said blandly, ignoring Harvey's expression.

Harvey grimaced. 'Now why did you come over here, old buddy?' he asked in a mock-aggressive tone.

'So you could buy me a drink,' remarked Nicholas complacently. 'Run along . . . old buddy.'

Harvey sighed and looked regretfully at Madeline.

'So be it. We all have our crosses to bear,' he remarked soulfully, causing Madeline to laugh at his injured manner, as he walked away.

After he had left them, Madeline twisted her glass nervously between her fingers, feeling tongue-tied. She was aware that he was studying her thoughtfully, and then he said:

'You're not annoyed that I broke up your conversation with Harvey, are you?'

Madeline looked up and shook her head vigorously.

'Heavens, no! I only met him about half an hour ago.'

'I see. I thought perhaps that you were his latest conquest.'

Madeline smiled. 'Oh, no. Nothing like that.'

'Good.' Nicholas looked serious and drew out his cigarette case. 'Do you smoke?' After she had taken one he went on: 'And your husband? Is he here tonight?'

'No. My husband died nine years ago.'

'Nine?' He looked very surprised. 'Forgive me, but I thought you were newly married.'

'Oh, please,' Madeline sighed. 'I'm thirty-three. Don't say I look like a teenager, please.'

He smiled. She was refreshingly different. Women of her age usually liked to be thought very young. It was his experience that women never liked to be thought the age they really were. The very young ones liked to be thought older and experienced, and the older ones spent all their time trying to recapture a youth which simply emphasized their actual ages.

'All right,' he agreed mildly. 'But you are a very attractive woman. And I think I ought to apologize for my rather churlish behaviour last week. I was not very polite. I'm sorry. I assure you I am not usually so ungallant. However, had we not met this evening, I should have definitely made an effort to discover your address and make some atonement.'

'That's not necessary,' murmured Madeline, feeling out of her depth.

'I must disagree. That afternoon I had had a rather disturbing telephone call from my daughter before leaving the factory and I'm afraid I was in quite an angry frame of mind.'

'That's all right,' replied Madeline, her heart sinking unreasonably at the mention of his daughter. She might have known he would be married. 'Is . . . is your wife over here with you?'

'My wife, also, is dead,' he replied with a shrug. 'She died when Maria was born, all of fifteen years ago.'

'I see.' Madeline bent her head. 'I have a daughter, too. She's a year older, sixteen.'

'Really?' He looked astounded. 'Maria is still in Rome. She wants to come over here and join me. Of course, she objects to my long absences abroad and as she lives with my mother she's rather spoiled and usually gets what she wants.'

'Do you intend being here long?' asked Madeline, looking up again.

He made an undecided gesture. 'Two months; three maybe. I've only been here ten days. I can't tell. If I like it here I may stay on.'

Harvey arrived back just then with a tray of drinks. He was not as tall as Nicholas, although he was a tall man, and they both seemed giants compared to the men Madeline was used to associating with.

They all stood talking together for a while and then presently were joined by Con Masterson and another young couple who were introduced as Paul and Mary-Lee Lucas. Mary-Lee chattered away easily to Madeline, asking her if she had any children and explaining that she herself had four. Madeline envied her her complete lack of self-consciousness.

Madeline herself still felt rather bemused by the whole affair. Con Masterson was now talking seriously to Nicholas Vitale and he was listening intently, now and then drawing on the cigarette between his fingers. Even in profile he was a remarkably handsome man, his eyelashes long and thick and very black. She wasn't sure whether she felt glad or sorry that their conversation was ended. She had enjoyed talking to him, but it was probably just as well that Harvey had come back. After all, it was obvious that Nicholas Vitale was perfectly at his ease with women and his charming manner was too expert to be assumed. No, he had had plenty of practice, while she was a mere novice when conversing with men.

Adrian came to join them later. Madeline was ashamed to realize that for a while she had forgotten all about him and Mr. Hetherington. He took Madeline's arm and said:

'You seem to be enjoying yourself.'

Nicholas, seeing the other man's rather possessive attitude towards Madeline, said:

'Tell me, Con, is the schoolmaster you were telling me about here?'

Con nodded. 'One of them,' he replied amiably. 'I'll introduce you.'

So Adrian found himself speaking to the owner of the factory and the large organization it represented. Madeline could tell from his expression that he was highly delighted and she wondered how large a part Nicholas Vitale's money played in Adrian's interest.

'Tell me,' said Nicholas, with interest, 'how old are the pupils who attend your school? Is it a large school?'

'The pupils range from eleven to eighteen years,' said Adrian, quite prepared to talk about his favourite subject. 'We have about eight hundred pupils altogether.'

'I see. My daughter Maria is fifteen. She is apparently not very interested in school at all. We have trouble in even getting her there. It occurs to me that school in England might not be a bad thing. Boarding school, of course.'

'Of course,' murmured Adrian, rather disheartened. He had half thought Vitale was going to suggest sending Maria to Otterbury.

'Do you have any school in mind you could recommend?' queried Nicholas Vitale, watching Adrian keenly.

Adrian spread wide his hands. 'I'm afraid I know very little about boarding schools in general. Would you send her to one of the better girls' schools or would you prefer mixed?'

Nicholas smiled. 'I think Maria had better have her say in that,' he remarked. 'If indeed she agrees to attend school over here, I think the least I can do is to let her choose her own school, don't you?'

'Oh, in that case. . . naturally.' Adrian compressed his lips. Madeline watching him, hazarded a guess that he considered that kind of attitude utterly wrong. Adrian always advocated that children never knew what was best for them and it was up to the adults to make the decisions.

'Won't she miss seeing you, if she's at school over here and you're in Italy?' she asked, unable to deny the question.

Nicholas Vitale's blue eyes met hers for a moment and she found herself feeling as though she had just run a race and could hardly get her breath. She could not draw her eyes away and it was only when he continued speaking and looked at someone else that she was able to gather her scattered wits. Why, she was as impressionable as a child herself and she forced herself not to look at him again.

But it was terribly difficult, particularly as she was fascinated by everything he said and did!

'I should imagine I could make time to come over and see her,' he said, in answer to Madeline's question. 'Besides, my mother wants to go to America for several months this year and it will relieve her of the responsibility of Maria if she is away too.'

Adrian was nodding in agreement and Madeline twisted her fingers together. If Maria came to school in England it was likely that Nicholas Vitale would be often in this country, and what better place to stay than near the factory? She might see him again!

Inwardly she was chiding herself for her lack of sophistication, but outwardly she looked calm. How ridiculous to even consider herself a suitable candidate for his interest. Besides, rich and powerful as he was, it was hardly likely that he would expect any woman to do any other than to fall over themselves to become closer associated with him. Any interest he might show in her could only be of a passing nature and although the prospect now might be appealing, when it was all over she would be the one who was hurt.

Anyway, she was a respectable widow with a daughter of impressionable age. She could imagine Diana's scandalized expression if she informed her she was considering having an affair with an Italian millionaire! Really, it was laughable, and he had not even asked her for a date! And yet something about the way he looked at her made her feel sure he would!

Hetherington came to join them and to find out what it was all about. He, much more than Adrian, could advise Nicholas Vitale on the choice of schools available to Maria and took the opportunity of getting his opinion voiced.

The conversation droned on, leaving Madeline to her own thoughts. She was unaware that Nicholas Vitale's gaze often strayed in her direction or that he wished the others would go and leave them to talk. It was years since he had found a woman more than passably interesting. Women usually served their purpose and were forgotten. Conversation with them was limited. Fashion, style, the latest hairdo, current drinking habits; these were the shallow topics he had grown used to. Madeline Scott was not like that, he was sure.

Madeline, listening occasionally to his voice, found it distinctly disturbing. Deep and husky, it gave you the feeling that what he was saying was for your ears alone.

In truth Nicholas was becoming increasingly bored with the whole affair. Admittedly, he wanted to get to know Madeline better, but this circle of would-be confidants surrounding him were beginning to jar and he wanted to be free of them.

Stubbing out his cigarette in a nearby ashtray, he broke up the conversation by saying:

'Thank you all for your advice. I'll certainly mention it to Maria when I see her.'

Madeline was shaken out of her lethargy at these words.

'Are . . . are you returning to Italy?' she exclaimed, the words bubbling out uncontrollably.

His eyes were gentle as he looked at her. 'No. Maria is coming here. My mother is staying on in Rome to clear things up and then she too will join us.'

'Oh!' Madeline drew back into her shell.

'Do you have a house, then?' asked Hetherington, in surprise.

'No. I have a suite at the Stag,' replied Nicholas dryly. This questioning was beginning to sound like the third degree.

The Stag was the largest hotel in Otterbury. Luxurious, opulent, it catered for people like Vitale and had been built at the same time as the factory site became operational. A very shrewd move on the part of the owners, who guessed correctly that there would be people coming to Otterbury who required more than the average in hotels. The locals in Otterbury could not afford its expensive food and drink and consequently no undesirable element was allowed within its portals.

Lucie Masterson came over then and really broke things up, much to Nicholas's relief. She looked coyly at him and said:

'Nick darling, you really ought to circulate more. It's so delightful having you here. We never see you these days . . .' this last said rather reproachfully.

Madeline, watching Nicholas Vitale's reactions, wondered how close Lucie would like to be to her husband's employer or whether indeed there had once been something between them. There was something about Lucie's attitude that suggested such a thing, and Madeline felt a trifle nauseated.

Nicholas shrugged his broad shoulders and glanced at

his watch.

'I'm sorry, Lucie,' he said coolly. 'I am rather a busy man.'

'You work far too hard,' she retorted, in annoyance. 'You ought to relax more.'

Nicholas looked down at her and Madeline could see his eyes had narrowed.

'How do you know I don't?' he said, rather deliberately, and Lucie stiffened. Madeline looked away; she had seen enough.

Nicholas saw Madeline turn away, her glorious hair glowing in the soft lights. He intended speaking to her again before he left.

'You're impossible,' Lucie exclaimed, in a low, angry voice.

'Yes, I am, aren't I?' he remarked disinterestedly, and then: 'Excuse me. There's someone I want to have a word with.'

Nicholas crossed to Madeline's side. She was standing apart from the others, apparently deep in thought.

'Will you allow me to take you home?' he asked softly, his eyes intent, as she swung round to face him.

Madeline looked up, almost startled out of her wits. Her eyes grew enormous and she felt herself blushing again. It really was an annoying feeling, to know you could not control your colour. His thickly lashed eyes seemed to hypnotize her and all the revulsion she had felt about his association with Lucie sped away. She was sure he must be aware of the effect he was having upon her and she shivered involuntarily. Clasping her arms together, she said:

'I . . . er . . . I came with Adrian Sinclair.'

'I didn't ask who you came with,' he remarked, rather dryly. 'I asked whether I could take you home.'

'But . . . but Adrian expects me t . . . to go with him,' she stammered, feeling foolish.

'I see. And that is important to you?'

Was it important? Madeline felt trapped. She could not in all honesty say that Adrian was terribly important to her, other than in a purely friendly capacity, but on the other hand how much more did she owe to him than to this comparative stranger? She was undecided and definitely nervous. She wanted to plunge in and say she would be thrilled if he took her home, but something held her back. It was like being pulled two ways at once with equal intensity. And yet was it equal? If she were truthful with herself she would admit that the idea of going anywhere with Nicholas Vitale was in itself an excitement, and Adrian could never be exciting!

Nicholas was studying her solemnly as she wavered on the brink. Then he said in an amused voice: 'I'm sure if it takes that much thinking about, the answer must be "no".'

Madeline struggled to find words to explain her indecision. What must he be thinking of her?

'You're probably right,' she agreed, at last. 'It's simply that Adrian and I are old friends and I ought not to hurt his feelings.'

'What you really mean is that he is interested in you,' remarked Nicholas shrewdly.

'I suppose I do,' she admitted quietly. 'We've known one another for five years now.'

'And you have been a widow all that time, haven't you?' he asked.

'Yes.'

'Then I think he is either very stupid or you are very stubborn.'

Madeline smiled. 'The latter. No one could call Adrian stupid.'

Nicholas shrugged. 'And so? Where does this get us? Would you like to come with me? If there was no Sinclair to interfere, of course.'

Madeline ran a hand over her hair, rather restlessly. 'I ... I ... oh, I suppose so,' she said, sighing.

Nicholas was satisfied. 'Good. Then I will speak to Sinclair.'

'Oh, no, please.' Madeline stared at him imploringly. 'You would only give Adrian the wrong impression.'

'How's that?' He drew his slim cigarette case from his pocket and offered it to her. Madeline accepted one of the long cigarettes and then after they were lit she began:

'Adrian would never understand. . . .'

At that moment Adrian himself chose to join them. 'Are you ready to leave, Madeline?' he asked. 'Hetherington doesn't want to be too late as his wife is alone.'

Nicholas studied the other man for a moment, and then said:

'Do I take it that you are driving Hetherington home?'

Adrian frowned. 'That's correct.'

Nicholas turned to Madeline. 'Then I suggest that as Mrs. Scott is in no hurry to leave at the moment, I will see to it that she arrives home safely, relieving you of that responsibility.'

Adrian was astounded and looked it. He did not want to offend the Italian and alternatively Vitale had really left him no choice but to accept his offer. Only Madeline could alter the situation and he looked questioningly at her.

Madeline herself felt very guilty. This was a new venture for her and she was half afraid of the consequences. Even so, she was unable to say the words Adrian wanted to hear; that she would go with him, now, this minute.

'Very well,' said Adrian stiffly, when it became obvious that Madeline intended to stay. 'Are you sure you want to stay on, Madeline?'

Madeline managed a smile. 'I don't mind,' she murmured quietly. 'And it's very kind of Mr. Vitale to offer to take me home.'

'I see.' Adrian sounded unconvinced. He had seen them talking together and had wondered what was transpiring. Now he knew. He was deceived for one moment and he was surprised that Madeline, whom he had thought he knew so well, should act so foolishly. After all, she scarcely knew the other man and Adrian had already heard about the kind of reputation Nicholas Vitale was supposed to have. As he did not know about their accidental meeting the previous week it looked even worse to him. He would never have believed that his secretary could be so deceitful.

He hesitated only a moment longer and then turned abruptly and strode away to where Hetherington was waiting for him. Madeline felt even more guilty now and rather mean. With a sigh she turned to Nicholas.

'I'm sorry, Mr. Vitale, but I'd better go with him. He'll be thinking I'm awfully ungrateful. After all, were it not for him, I shouldn't be here this evening.'

Nicholas put out a hand and detained her. His hard fingers encircled the yielding flesh of her upper arm and she felt herself weaken.

'Maybe not,' he said quietly, 'but now you are here and I want to take you home, and I usually get what I want. He'll get over it.' There was arrogance in his voice and she felt half annoyed.

'I can make up my own mind, thank you,' she replied stiffly.

'Can you? I wonder. Either way, it's too late now. He's gone.'

And so he had! After bidding farewell to his host and hostess, Adrian had left the room without a backward glance. The decision had been made for her.

Feeling a nervous apprehension descend upon her, Madeline looked about her. The exquisitely furnished room was full of strangers. Even the man beside her was a stranger. She must be completely mad! Adrian would certainly think so.

She was aware that Nicholas Vitale's hand was still holding her arm and she looked up at him, her eyes questioning. Just as he returned her gaze Harvey turned round to speak to them and immediately she was free. She rubbed her arm where he had held it, and felt her blood pounding through her veins.

'Have you enjoyed yourself, then?' asked Harvey, his eyes dancing.

Madeline gave a small smile. 'Very much, thank you.'

Harvey grinned, 'You sound like a little girl thanking her teacher for the Sunday school treat!'

'I'm sorry.' Madeline straightened her shoulders. 'Actually, it's been quite a new experience for me.'

'You must repeat the experience again, soon,' said Harvey easily. 'There are usually a few unattached males like myself at these gatherings who enjoy having an attractive woman to talk to.' He grimaced openly at Nicholas.

Madeline herself glanced surreptitiously in Nicholas Vitale's direction, but he was now talking to another man who had joined them and they seemed thoroughly absorbed in their own conversation.

'Did I hear aright?' went on Harvey, in a low voice. 'Is Nick really taking you home?'

'That's right.' She shrugged her slim shoulders. 'Why do you ask?'

Harvey gave a low whistle. 'My, my,' he said admiringly. 'You certainly are a brave little girl. Taking on Nick is a different proposition from taking on me. Watch your step. Nick eats little girls like you for breakfast.'

'Oh, don't be ridiculous,' exclaimed Madeline, aware with every moment that passed that she had been a fool not to leave with Adrian. She was out of her depth here. These were not her kind of people. She was not even in their income bracket for a start. And Harvey's teasing simply annoyed her now. 'I'm quite capable of taking care of myself, thank you.'

'Are you, indeed?' Harvey looked sceptical.

Madeline looked again at Nicholas Vitale. He was explaining some facet of technical car design to the other man and was demonstrating with his lean, tanned fingers the size of the component he was describing. Madeline felt her heart miss a beat. She wondered how it would feel to have those hands touching her, caressing her. Something about this man drew her tremendously and it was frightening to feel this way. Until now, no man, and certainly not Joe, had affected her like this. It was a strange new experience. She was becoming aware of sensations

54

about herself she had not even known existed.

As though sensing her scrutiny, Nicholas suddenly looked across at her. Seeing the rather tensed expression on her face, he murmured:

'Do you want to leave now?'

Madeline looked about her helplessly. 'Well ... I ... don't let me distract you from your conversation. I can easily get a taxi.' Inside her she felt she had got to get away from here, and fast! She was panicking, she knew, but was unable to stop herself.

Nicholas Vitale frowned, his brows drawn together in an angry line.

'That won't be necessary,' he replied coolly. 'Harvey, will you explain to Belmont about the new distributor head?'

Harvey shrugged his shoulders. 'Okay, Nick. Will I see you in the morning?'

'Sure. I'll be in early. I have to go to the airport later to meet Maria.'

'Okay,' Harvey grinned, and winked at Madeline, but she was in no mood to appreciate his humour. To her mind, there was no humour in this situation.

The Mastersons looked surprised to see them leaving together. Madeline thought that Lucie Masterson looked positively venomous as she said good-bye to the younger woman. She had adopted a possessive attitude with Nicholas earlier, but it was plain to see that whatever she would like to think, Nicholas had no interest in her.

Madeline was glad when they got outside. She had put on her coat in the hall and Nicholas had donned a short camel coat. It was raining heavily as they hurried across the courtyard to where a low-slung white saloon was parked. It, too, was a Sheridan, but of a different type from the red one.

He helped her inside and then walked round and slid in beside her. The seats were wide and luxurious and superbly comfortable. Madeline felt herself relaxing and lay back lazily in her seat.

Nicholas's coat collar was up and although he turned

on the engine, before moving away he turned towards her. Madeline thought he really was a most devastatingly handsome man, and her heart leapt into her throat.

'Why did you say you would take a taxi?' he asked abruptly.

Madeline was shaken out of her placidity. 'I thought you were involved and I didn't want to disturb you,' she replied, feeling as nervous as a kitten.

He looked sceptical. He had switched on the interior light now and she was aware of looking as guilty as could be.

'Well, honestly,' she cried, 'I'm just an ordinary widow with no pretensions to beauty, with a daughter who is nearly grown-up. Of what possible interest can I be to you? I'm not your type, at all.'

Nicholas shrugged, almost imperceptibly, and then switched off the light. The car moved swiftly down the drive and out on to the Otterbury road. They moved effortlessly along and Madeline wondered whether she would ever feel normal again.

'Why should you imagine I am interested in you?' he asked slowly.

Madeline felt as though her knees were shaking and she hoped he would not notice. His remarks were disconcerting to say the least and she did not know how to answer him. She decided to ignore his question and said:

'I live not far from here. It's the next turning on your right. It's really quite near Ingleside. If you stop at the end of the road I can easily walk up. . . .'

He did not reply, but the car curved into the Gardens and drove on.

'These are the flats,' she managed to say in a small voice, and he stopped the car instantly. The Gardens were deserted; the downpour had deterred anyone from leaving the comfort of their homes.

Madeline fumbled with her handbag and gloves, preparatory to getting out, but he said deliberately: 'You didn't answer my question.'

She was glad the light was not on at that moment. Darkness was friendly and unrevealing and she was sure her face was like a tomato.

'No . . . did you expect an answer?'

'Of course.' He turned towards her, his thigh brushing hers as he did so. 'I want to know.'

She was certain now that he was conscious of the effect he was having on her. His nearness was breathtaking and exhilarating, and although she knew she ought to feel angry with him, all she felt was an overwhelming sense of longing for a closer contact.

'I think you're teasing me,' she said, at last, trying rather unsuccessfully to introduce a lighter vein.

'No, I am not.' He looked amused.

She had never dreamed any man could be so disturbing. She had never in her life before had to deal with a situation like this. Her life had, in many ways, been sheltered and Nicholas Vitale was an entirely unknown quantity.

'Tell me,' he murmured, 'are you scared? Is that why you're trembling? What has Harvey been saying to you?'

His arm was along the back of the seat behind her and his fingers closed on her shoulder, stilling the trepidation she was feeling.

'N . . . N . . . Nothing,' she stammered, her whole being alight with emotion; an emotion caused by the touch of his hand.

'I'm sure he has said something,' he remarked, studying her profile in the light from the street lamp.

He was so close to her she could smell the clean, male fragrance about him, the indefinable maleness enhanced by good tobacco and shaving cream. He was deliberately challenging her, making her wholly aware of herself as a woman and she felt warm all over.

'I must go,' she said firmly, and put her hand on the door handle. Nicholas leaned past her and prevented her from opening it. He did not intend letting her go, just like that. In a short space of time she had aroused feelings in him which he had thought permanently dormant.

'Not yet,' he murmured softly. 'I want to know when I will see you again.'

Madeline stared at him. 'Are you serious?'

He frowned momentarily. 'Sure I'm serious. Did you imagine I would drive you home and walk out of your life, as simple as that?'

'I don't know. You might have imagined I was ... well....'

'Easy?' he supplied softly. 'I never thought that for a moment. Now, when?'

'I can't think why you want to see *me*, then.'

'Can't you?' He smiled almost mockingly. 'No, perhaps not. For a woman who has been married, you're incredibly naïve.'

'Thank you,' said Madeline, her voice a little hurt.

'Well, it is a compliment in many ways,' he remarked softly. 'Do you know you're a very desirable woman?'

Madeline shivered. 'I'm just an ordinary housewife, who has to go to work,' she said, with a sigh.

'Not to me,' he murmured, his fingers twisting a curl of amber hair. 'Come on, honey. Tomorrow night, hmn?'

'I don't know.' Madeline was having difficult in articulating.

'Why not? Don't fence, Madeline. That's not necessary between us. I want you to come and I know you want to come. It's as simple as that. You're as damned well disturbed by me as I am by you.'

'I ... I disturb you?' She stared at him.

His eyes were dark and unreadable, but she could sense the power behind the words. His fingers tightened convulsively about her shoulders for a moment and then he released her.

'Stop baiting me,' he muttered. 'Now, tomorrow night. What time?'

'My daughter might not approve,' she murmured, her resistance ebbing.

'That's too bad.' There was arrogance in his voice again. 'Look, I'll pick you up here at seven-thirty, right?'

'Oh, all right.' Madeline bent her head. She was power-less to refuse.

'Good.' Taking a handful of her hair, he pulled her head back and looked down into her face. 'Be punctual,' he muttered.

Madeline's lips were parted as she stared at him and he groaned:

'Don't make me touch you, honey, or I won't let you go.'

Madeline drew her head away from him and slid out of the car all in one movement. To her surprise he slid out too and they stood together for a moment in the rain.

'Don't forget,' he murmured softly, all the arrogance gone from him now.

'As if I could!' she whispered helplessly, and ran swiftly into the apartment building.

CHAPTER FOUR

DIANA was sitting in an armchair, reading, when Madeline let herself in. She looked up smiling at her mother.

'Isn't Uncle Adrian with you?'

Madeline removed her damp coat before replying. She still felt rather shaken and found difficulty in speaking and acting as though nothing untoward had occurred.

'I didn't come home with Adrian, darling,' she answered slowly. 'He left a little earlier to take Mr. Hetherington home and I came with someone else.'

Diana looked suspicious and Madeline wondered guiltily what she would think if she could read her mother's thoughts at that moment.

'Who?' Diana asked at once.

Madeline smoothed her hair nervously. 'Mr. Vitale, darling.'

Diana frowned. The name was familiar. Of course – that was the name of the man who owned the new factory. She looked flabbergasted.

'Vitale? You mean the one from the factory?'

'That's right.' Madeline hoped she was smiling brightly. 'Wasn't that a surprise? Have you had supper?'

Diana did not reply to her question but rose to her feet. 'Mum, have you and Uncle Adrian had a row?'

Madeline flushed. 'Of course not. Don't be silly. I'm not responsible to Adrian for my movements, am I?'

Diana looked more suspicious than ever. This was a most peculiar affair as far as she could see. Her mother had never departed for the evening with one man and returned home with another in the past. Come to think of it, Uncle Adrian was the only man Diana could ever remember her mother going out with, since Daddy died.

'Did you enjoy yourself, then?' she asked politely.

'Oh, yes. It was very interesting,' replied Madeline inadequately. 'There were quite a lot of Americans there too.'

'This Mr. Vitale – he's Italian, of course?'

'Of course. Not that I know much about him, but I think he is.'

'Oh!' Diana shook her head. She didn't understand all this, but Madeline determined to change the subject. As for the following evening's engagement, she dreaded to think how she was going to introduce that without causing more embarrassment.

'I see you did wash your hair,' she remarked, walking into the kitchen briskly to make the coffee for supper.

'Yes.' Diana sighed and flung herself back in the chair. She was still pondering over her mother's actions, although it was apparent that Madeline did not want to talk about it. Diana thought she looked different too. Younger somehow, and much less sure of herself. Diana did not like it. What was this man really like who had brought her home? Was he young or old? And why had he decided to bring her mother? Surely he couldn't be interested in her.

Diana swallowed hard. No, she was definitely making a mountain out of a molehill. After all, if this man lived in town it was logical to suppose that he had simply offered to drop Madeline off here on his way.

The following morning they slept in. Madeline was late for school and dreaded meeting Adrian after last night's episode. He would be bound to demand an explanation of her actions and she hadn't one to give him. She could hardly say she had gone home with Nicholas Vitale because she had felt an immediate attraction towards him.

And she still hadn't told Diana about the evening. Really, life was becoming increasingly complicated.

She seated herself at her desk and began typing diligently. Lessons began at nine-thirty, but the school assembled in the hall prior to this for morning prayers.

Adrian conducted the prayers and did not usually return to his office until after the first period.

Today, however, he returned immediately after prayers. Madeline was engrossed in the schedules he had left her the previous evening and hoped he would not tackle her on private matters until later in the day. But she was doomed to disappointment, Adrian came straight into her office and walked purposefully up to her desk.

'Well,' he said. 'So you got home safely?'

'Naturally.' Madeline managed a smile. 'It was an interesting evening, wasn't it?'

'Enormously,' said Adrian with some sarcasm.

'Now look,' said Madeline, deciding to take the bull by the horns, 'you're in no position to criticize my actions.'

Adrian snorted. 'If our relationship was purely a business one, which it's not, I should still feel obliged to warn you about Vitale.'

'Warn me?' Madeline stared at him.

'Yes, warn you. Madeline, Nicholas Vitale is a man of the world. Good lord, he's not a man for you to play around with. Let him confine himself to his own kind. They won't object to his actions.'

'Oh, really, Adrian! Mr. Vitale only took me home.'

'Maybe. But he could have ... well ... shall we say, molested you.'

'He could have what?' Madeline almost laughed. 'What an old-fashioned expression, Adrian! Besides, I hardly think Mr. Vitale has to employ those tactics with his physical attributes.'

Adrian stiffened his shoulders. 'My dear Madeline, I have always considered you a sane and sensible woman; one indeed with whom I should like to share my life, but since last evening you seem to have changed into an irresponsible schoolgirl and I'm deeply disappointed in you.'

'But why?'

'Because, although you've been married, your marriage seems to me to have been quite unique. You were so young and although I suppose you had your reasons for marrying Joe, and I don't want to intrude on your private affairs, I do think you're not experienced in the ways of men. Nicholas Vitale is far different from Joe, who seems to have placed you on a pedestal and worshipped you from afar, as they say. You seem so – untouched. You have an innocent appearance which I've always admired. I know you have a child, but I don't think passion has ever touched you. I know Vitale is physically attractive, but you have no idea of the raw, animalistic tendencies that are apparent in some men.'

Madeline interrupted him hotly. She looked and felt very embarrassed. 'Please, Adrian, don't go on. I don't want to hear any more.'

'I'm quite sure you don't,' he agreed, frowning. 'Which only goes to prove that you think you know what you're doing.'

'But what am I doing? I only came home with him, didn't I?'

'And are you seeing him again?'

She shrugged, as casually as she could. 'I don't know,' she murmured awkwardly.

Adrian looked disbelievingly at her but did not contradict her.

'Madeline, my dear, I don't want to see you hurt. My thoughts are only for you. You know that.'

Madeline sighed, and reached for her handbag. She extracted her cigarettes and lit one slowly. Everything Adrian had said was buzzing round in her mind and a lot of it was true. Was she so naïve? Did she appear ridiculously vulnerable? After all, even Nicholas Vitale had said she was naïve, and that after only one evening's acquaintance. And now, the idea of going out with him this evening was beginning to loom frighteningly on the horizon. Might it not be better to ring him and cancel the whole thing now? If Adrian was wholly right about him he was only amusing himself anyway and she knew she couldn't react to a situation like that as he might expect her too. She was no fly-by-night evening's entertainment. She was a serious person at heart and she had no intention of indulging in a tawdry affair however exciting it might seem at the time. As she pondered on these things, memories of Joe flooded back to her. His gentleness; his unemotional tenderness; the love he had so selflessly given her when she had had none to give in return. Instinctively she knew that Nicholas Vitale would take as much as he gave, passionately, and there would be nothing gentle or undemanding about it.

'It's nine-thirty,' she said, at last, glancing at her watch. 'Your class will be waiting for you.'

Adrian sighed impatiently. 'Oh, very well. We'll have to talk later.'

Madeline did not look up as he left the room. She determined that there would be no more talks today. She had had as much of that as she could take.

That evening Diana was home before Madeline and had laid the table before her mother entered the flat. She looked amiable enough and seemed to have forgotten about the previous evening's unsettled ending. Madeline hoped that when she told her she was going out that Diana would remain amiable.

'Had a good day?' asked Diana, watching her mother light a cigarette.

'Reasonably so,' replied Madeline awkwardly. 'Diana, would you mind if I went out this evening?' It came out with a rush and left Diana looking troubled.

'Went out? You mean with Uncle Adrian?'

'Well . . . no. Not exactly. With Mr. Vitale.'

Diana was nonplussed. 'Mr. Vitale?' she echoed.

Madeline nodded. Watching the expression on Diana's face her heart sank. Diana was not going to concede gracefully. She wondered then whether she had been too mindful of her daughter in the past. After all, she was still young. Other women went out with men at her age; some of them widows, others not even married and still others who were married and went out with other men. When Diana grew up and got married, she would not wish to feel obliged to consider her mother and then perhaps she would understand Madeline's position.

'But, Mother,' exclaimed Diana now, 'you hardly know him! And he's not even English. Besides, the girls at college say there's only one Vitale and he's the man who owns the factory.'

'That's right.' Madeline drew on her cigarette.

Diana swallowed hard. Her face was considerably redder and she looked very upset.

'But why?' she cried childishly. 'Why? Uncle Adrian won't approve, I'm sure.'

Madeline shrugged. 'Darling, don't fuss so. Uncle Adrian had nothing to do with it. He's only a friend. He's not my keeper.'

'He wants to marry you.'

'And I don't want to marry him,' said Madeline patiently. 'Diana, he's too old, too set in his ways.'

'He's no older than Daddy was.'

Madeline sighed. 'Maybe so, but that doesn't alter the facts.'

'And this Mr. Vitale. Is he like Daddy?'

'No. Not at all.'

'Then tell me what he is like. I have a right to know,' exclaimed Diana petulantly.

'Well, he's very nice,' said Madeline slowly. It was difficult to describe Nicholas Vitale without sounding as though it was being overdone. He was so dynamic, so confidently assured, so arrogant.

'Is he young or old?'

'Well, I suppose he's older than me,' said Madeline thoughtfully.

'Pretty old, then,' remarked Diana, rather spitefully.

Madeline did not reply. She supposed that to Diana she did seem old. It was no use arguing with her. She didn't want her to fly into a tantrum as she had done occasionally in the past.

'Well, I'm sure you're going to like him,' she said, trying to sound convincing.

'I'm equally sure I shan't,' retorted Diana, and stalked away into the kitchen.

Madeline ate very little of the casserole she had prepared that morning. She wasn't hungry, and besides, Nicholas Vitale would probably expect her to eat a meal. She wished she had not agreed to go out with him. Diana was in a black mood and had hardly spoken since their conversation before the meal. If there was to be this upheaval every time she suggested going out, she would rather take the line of least resistance and stay in.

But when it was time to get ready she found she was determined to look her best. She wore a black lace cocktail dress which she had had for several years. Originally it had been an expensive model and its sheath line and low round neckline did not age. Her only string of pearls was around her throat. Joe had bought them ten years ago for an anniversary present and although they were only imitation they looked real enough.

She wore the cream wool coat again and was almost ready to go down to meet him at seven-twenty-five when the door-bell rang.

Diana was staying in for the evening and was in the lounge at the time. She went to open the door, wondering who it could be. A tall, broad-shouldered man confronted her. He was very dark-skinned and was dressed in a sheepskin jacket over a dark suit. He had the bluest eyes of anyone she had ever met and they looked bluer than ever against his tanned skin. His shirt was white and he wore a tie which was obviously that of some well-known educational establishment. His hair was blue-black and curly and his eyelashes were long and curled too. He was quite unique in a town like Otterbury where money and good looks never went together and Diana was absolutely astonished. Could this be the man her mother was going out with?

'Yes?' she said, in a small, cold voice. She was still hoping against hope that he would turn out to be somebody else entirely.

The man smiled and said: 'Are you Madeline's daughter? I guess you must be, at that.'

'That's right. I'm Diana. Are you Mr. Vitale?'

66

Before he could reply, Madeline's voice called, 'Who is it, darling?' and she emerged from the bedroom in her stockinged feet, her hair curling delicately about her face. When she saw Nicholas her face changed, and she felt her stomach lurch dizzily. 'Hello,' she murmured. 'Won't you come in?'

Diana stood aside, still feeling rather dazed. Nicholas Vitale was so unlike anything she had even imagined. In her wildest dreams she had never contemplated anyone like him being interested in her mother, and he was far from being old. She felt a kind of sick panic when she considered them together. This man was not like Uncle Adrian, who treated her mother exactly like an old acquaintance. This man would very likely demand a much more intimate relationship. The idea horrified and frightened her and she wished desperately that something could happen to prevent their date.

Nicholas stepped into the flat, immediately dwarfing it. He looked about him with interest, approving the blue and white decor. It was bright and modern and uncluttered.

'You've met Diana, I see,' said Madeline, hastily slipping her feet into her court shoes. 'Diana darling, this is Mr. Vitale.'

'I know.' Diana was guarded.

Madeline looked appealingly at Nicholas and he said:

'Are you still at school, Diana?'

Diana shrugged. 'I'm at commercial college,' she replied indifferently.

'Do you like it?'

'Sometimes.' Diana swung round and flopped on to an armchair.

Nicholas looked thoughtful. Diana did not intimidate him and nor did her attitude appeal to him. In his opinion, Diana needed a lesson in manners and he felt like being the one to give it to her. Madeline was looking anxious and upset and he felt like giving Diana a piece of his mind. After all, whatever his reputation might be, Diana knew none of it, and she ought to know that her mother was a decent, honest woman. Woman; he half-smiled. Madeline was little more than a girl herself. He had felt the same immediate reaction at the sight of her and he inwardly chided himself for allowing his feelings to run away with his thoughts.

'Are you ready?' Nicholas looked at Madeline, his eyes warm and tender, and she felt the colour flame into her cheeks.

'Yes, I'm ready,' she murmured. She turned to Diana. 'Are you sure you'll be all right? I shan't be late.'

'I'll be all right.' Diana scarcely looked up from the magazine she was glancing through. 'Don't bother to hurry back. I can put myself to bed.'

Madeline bit her lip. Diana was genuinely trying to hurt her, and she was succeeding. The evening was being spoilt before it had begun.

They went downstairs to his car. It was warm and comfortable and as he drove expertly down Evenwood Gardens and out on to the main road, Madeline tried to relax and forget Diana's harsh words. But her silence infuriated Nicholas and he said angrily:

'I gather I'm not very popular with your daughter. Why?'

Madeline shrugged. 'Diana doesn't understand why I don't marry Adrian Sinclair. As far as she's concerned, anyone over the age of twenty-five is in their dotage and any man would do, providing she approved of him.'

'But not me,' he muttered. 'Why?'

'I ... oh ... I don't know. I'm her mother....'

He smiled. 'You don't look old enough to be anybody's mother.'

'Maybe not, but I am. Perhaps that's part of the trouble.'

They drove through Otterbury to the Stag Hotel. As they did so, Madeline recalled that his daughter had arrived from Italy today. She wondered whether she would be having dinner with them.

They parked the car and then walked into the hotel. Nicholas took her to the residents' bar and ordered a

Martini cocktail for her and a bourbon for himself.

They sat on stools at the bar and after he had lit their cigarettes he said:

'You look very beautiful, Mrs. Scott.'

'Thank you, Mr. Vitale.' She felt herself relax more fully. She was enjoying herself. Only the memory of Diana marred her complete enjoyment.

He smiled rather wryly. 'I'm very glad you came.'

She frowned. 'Did you think I might not?'

'Well, I guessed there might be some pressure on somebody's part to stop you. This Sinclair chap, for example, I'm surprised he didn't get in your hair.'

Madeline laughed softly. 'Oh, Adrian had his say all right. He advised me not to see you again.'

'I see. Has he the right to advise you?'

'Not really.'

'Well, that only leaves us with Diana. I guess her feelings are understandable when I think about it.'

'Why?' Madeline looked at him.

'Diana is at the age to understand sufficient about the physical needs of a man and woman to know that we are attracted to one another. She was surprised to find you going out with a man who she imagines will make love to you.' Madeline bent her head to hide her embarrassment. He went on softly: 'It frightens her a little. She's never had anything like this to contend with before. If Adrian is a sample of your previous men friends, this problem will never have arisen.'

'Adrian is the only man I've been out with since Joe died,' put in Madeline slowly.

'Okay. So that's the picture. It's rather unsettling for her. You won't find Maria at all like that. She's not a bit like Diana.'

'I see. And what exactly are my needs, my physical needs?' She said it lightly, but his eyes grew warm and caressing.

'I'll explain later,' he murmured lazily, and was amused at her shocked countenance.

Their conversation veered into less personal channels

69

after that. Nicholas was an amusing companion and he told her about his home in Rome and about the business which he had inherited from his late father. He had visited many countries and Madeline was intrigued.

After they had finished their second drinks they left the bar and walked across the residents' hall to the lifts. The private dining-room was on the left and Madeline looked puzzled.

'Where are we going?' she asked.

'To my suite,' he said imperturbably. 'Relax. We're having dinner up there. It's much nicer.'

'Oh!' Madeline was speechless for a moment. Then she said: 'But I'm not sure that I. . . .'

He sighed and shook his head. 'Don't be prudish. God, I'm not going to attack you, you know.'

'I'm sorry.' Madeline looked subdued, and Nicholas looked rather angrily at her.

The lift arrived and going up Madeline suddenly remembered Maria. Of course, his daughter would be dining with them. That was why they were going up to his suite.

The corridor was carpeted, and led past several doors before they reached Nicholas's suite of rooms. Inside it was magnificent and Madeline gasped in amazement. The ceilings were high and vaulted, elaborately carved. Marble pillars supported the alcoves and tall vases of glorious red hothouse roses were everywhere. The walls were hung with gold and silver damask while the furniture was satin-covered and luxurious. The carpet was a creamy golden colour while the curtains at the tall windows were of silver embossed velvet. Madeline had never been in a room like it before and it was some minutes before she realized that it was empty.

Nicholas had removed his coat after closing the doors and stood behind her, amused at her gasping wonderment.

'I gather it meets with your approval,' he remarked dryly, and she spun round to face him.

'It's like a film set,' she murmured, spreading wide her

hands. 'I can hardly believe I'm actually here. Am I dreaming?'

'No.' He smiled. 'Take off your coat.'

Madeline ran a tongue over her lips. 'I thought your daughter was due to arrive today.'

'That's right. She did. Why?'

'Where is she?'

'In her room, I should think,' he replied, frowning a little. 'What do you want to drink?'

As he crossed the room to the elaborate tray of drinks Madeline pressed a hand to her stomach. 'I don't think I should have any more. I'm not used to drinking alcohol.'

'Rubbish. One more won't hurt you.' He poured her another Martini and turned round again. He saw she had not removed her coat and stood down the glasses on a nearby tray and crossed to her side. He lifted the coat from her shoulders and laid it over one of the chairs. Then he turned back to her and his eyes were serious.

'Honey, I can read you like an open book. Maria has her own suite of rooms on the first floor, further along this corridor. If she were in my suite we would be continually on top of one another. She has a maid and a companion, you see.'

'Oh! Well, aren't all these doors the entrances to bedrooms?'

'Four of them are. The others are bathrooms. Would you like to look around?'

Madeline shrugged. She still felt wary and he was conscious of it. 'All right,' he said, 'come on. I have something to show you anyway.'

He flung open the door which led into the master bedroom and gently pushed her into the room. 'There. How do you like that?'

The master bedroom was a massive size, but was dominated by an enormous double bed which must have been at least six feet wide and seven feet long. The ceiling above the bed was carved with cupids, each sporting a tiny bow-and-arrow, and the heavy white satin draperies

71

over the bed were looped up to the ceiling to be let down for complete privacy if the bed was used.

'I imagine this is the bridal suite,' remarked Nicholas, half-laughingly. 'Can you imagine me sleeping in that?'

Madeline smiled up at him. 'Not really.'

'Well ... not alone,' he murmured, her eyes rousing him to awareness of their isolation here. He forced himself to look away from her and said: 'Come on, I'll show you my room.'

He opened another door to reveal quite a masculine room, carpeted in dark green with heavy furniture and a green bedspread, not a bit opulent like the room next door.

'The bed's comfortable,' he remarked mockingly. 'I must admit, I like a comfortable bed.'

Madeline turned away in embarrassment. To picture Nicholas in bed was a disturbing thought and she felt her hands clench involuntarily.

'And now,' he said, 'I've a present for you.'

'For me?' Madeline looked surprised.

'Of course.' He lifted a box from a side table and put it into her hands. 'I thought it would be better to give you these when we were alone. I don't think Diana would have appreciated the thought.'

Nestling in its cellophane box was a spray of orchids, the petals creamy and tinged with a tawny red which matched her hair. Madeline had never received such beautiful, or expensive, flowers and her fingers trembled as she lifted the spray out of the box.

'They're lovely!' she exclaimed, looking up at him. 'Thank you so much.'

He shrugged and said: 'Pin them on your dress. They should look perfect then.'

'Thank you again,' Madeline smiled, and did as he suggested.

A knock at the door heralded the arrival of two waiters with trolleys on which was the dinner Nicholas had ordered. A polished table was laid with table mats and sparkling silver and glassware, which was mirrored in the gleaming surface. The waiters stayed to serve the meal and Madeline felt intensely conscious of their scrutiny. She was sure they would realize she was unused to such deferential treatment and consequently her appetite dissolved and she ate very little. Nicholas was at his ease, tasting the different wines offered with each course, and generally assuming control. The food was superbly cooked and Madeline reflected that the chef here was certainly as adept as the chef at the Crown. She supposed the reason she and Adrian had never tried the Stag before was that it was usually fully booked for evening meals, well in advance.

They had grapefruit as an hors d'oeuvre, followed by a clear consommé which was spiced with sherry. Lemon sole with tartare sauce preceded chicken Marengo, which was chicken fried to a golden brown and served with sliced mushrooms, truffles and pastry crescents, in a delicious sauce. Finally they reached the dessert and Madeline gasped at the confection which was put before her. A strawberry trifle had been topped by whipped cream which in turn had been topped by shredded nuts and cherries. The result was more than Madeline could possibly manage and she finally sat back, replete.

The waiters removed the dishes and after serving coffee they left. Nicholas rose to his feet and crossed to the tray of drinks.

'Which liqueur would you like with your coffee?' he asked casually.

'Liqueur?' Madeline shook her head. 'I really don't think. . . .'

'Nonsense.' He smiled. 'I was going to suggest Green Chartreuse, but I think perhaps a fruit brandy might be less lethal.'

'So long as it is,' she answered, with a sigh. 'That really was a marvellous meal.'

'You ate very little,' he commented, handing her a glass of Maraschino.

Madeline looked regretful. 'I'm afraid I'm not used to

such close attention while I'm eating.'

'I see. It won't happen again, then. But did you prefer it to the formality of the restaurant?'

'Apart from that, yes.' She smiled. 'This is delicious.' She indicated the brandy.

'Good.' He walked round the table. 'Shall we sit on more comfortable seats?'

Madeline nodded and rose to her feet, and Nicholas drew back her chair. They crossed to one of the low loungers and Madeline sank down luxuriously on to the satin upholstery. To her surprise, Nicholas seated himself beside her and lay back looking at her, intently.

'Tell me more about yourself,' he said.

Madeline sat forward, and gave a light smile. 'There's nothing to tell. By the way, what time is it?'

Nicholas glanced at his watch. 'A quarter after nine.'

'Already?' Madeline was astounded. She had not been conscious of the passage of time and it seemed to have flown.

'It's early yet,' he remarked indolently. 'Don't change the subject. I want to know about Diana's father. What was he like?'

Madeline felt her hands grow clammy. Uneasiness probed its fingers into her system.

'You ... you mean ... Joe?'

'Naturally. Tell me about him. What was he like?'

Madeline stiffened her shoulders. 'Joe was just an ordinary person. . . .'

'What have you to hide?' exclaimed Nicholas impatiently, and Madeline shivered. He looked relaxed and yet she was sure his mind was as active as ever. He had the look of a preying animal when it is preparing to pounce.

'Nothing,' denied Madeline, at once, forcing a smile to her lips. 'It's simply that my affairs are very dull compared to the life you lead.'

Nicholas looked sceptical. She was convinced he did not believe her. But there again, there was nothing he could possibly suspect.

'You're on edge,' he remarked bluntly, and leaning forward he placed his empty glass on a nearby table. Madeline's eyes were drawn to him. His darkness itself was an attraction. She wondered whether his Italian blood gave him that animal appeal; that physical magnetism.

'I . . . er . . . I think I ought to be going,' she murmured. She bent her head for a moment, studying the gold band of her wedding ring. Unknown to her, her hair swung against her cheek like a silky curtain, veiling her face. She almost jumped out of her skin when she felt his fingers lift the hair and curl it back behind her ear. His hard fingers were cool and they brushed deliberately against her warm cheek.

She looked across at him. He looked as relaxed as ever, but now she knew he was not. His fingers left her cheek and curved caressingly round the nape of her neck, under her hair. His thumb moved in a circular movement, arousing her emotions and frightening her with their intensity. She was aware that his expertise came from considerable experience, but it did not change the effect he was having on her.

'Please,' she protested softly, putting up a hand to stop him. To her surprise he caught her hand in his and carried it to his lips, turning it over and kissing her palm with warm insistence.

'You're so scared,' he murmured, half-amused and half-impatient. 'Don't be. I won't hurt you.'

'I'm not scared!' she exclaimed hotly. 'Just because I don't swoon when you come near me and behave in a normal manner.'

'Come here, then,' he interrupted her quietly, his voice mocking.

Madeline rose to her feet abruptly, drawing her hand away from him. She realized she was scared, miserably so. Adrian was right. She was no match for Nicholas Vitale. He knew all the right answers. She didn't.

She half-expected him to rise too, but he simply remained negligently on the lounger and watched her agitated confusion.

'I suppose you think this is very amusing,' she said at last, her hands twisting together.

Nicholas shrugged. In truth he did not want to analyse his own feelings. Usually, he was quite willing to break down a woman's resistance simply by the force of his own personality. With Madeline he felt an almost violent need to protect her; from herself if need be.

'Sit down,' he said, leaning forward, legs apart.

Madeline shook her head. 'No. I must go.'

Nicholas at last rose to his feet and looked down on her. He was much taller than she was and she felt immediately at a disadvantage. Also, she was experiencing almost wanton feelings of desire for this man and she couldn't force her legs to move away and put the necessary distance between them.

When she looked up at him his eyes were dark and unfathomable and she thought there was a trace of amusement playing around his mouth.

'Well,' he murmured softly.

'Well what?' she asked, her quickened breathing almost stifling her.

He smiled and his hands gripped her shoulders and drew her close against him. She could feel the hardness of his body and she felt herself yield and lie against him. He bent his head and put his mouth to the side of her neck, its warm, caressing touch more heady than any of the wine she had drunk that evening. He kissed her shoulders, her throat, the soft nape of her neck, and Madeline was on fire for him to kiss her mouth. But he didn't.

Her arms slid up round his neck and she said: 'Please. Stop tormenting me,' in an aching voice.

He looked down at her, his face serious now, his eyes dark and yet demanding. Her lips parted and with a groan he bent his head and put his mouth to hers.

Madeline wound her arms tighter round his neck, pressing herself against him, glorying in the unexplored delights she was experiencing. Her passion matched his and she was unaware of his inner torment until he suddenly released her, and gently pushed her away from him.

'God!' he muttered, and walked slowly over to the tray of drinks. He poured himself a stiff whisky and after drinking it he turned round and leaned against the table, studying her. 'I was right,' he muttered. 'Madeline, I'm only human. Have you any idea how dangerous I could be?'

Madeline flushed under his scrutiny, but she did not look ashamed. She had realized, only too well, that she had never experienced this kind of lovemaking before, but she still remembered the last few minutes with a feeling of ecstasy.

'I don't think you frighten me any more,' she murmured softly, her eyes, dancing. 'On the contrary, I find you quite ... well ... stimulating.'

Nicholas gave a muffled exclamation and crossed the room to her side. Holding her firmly by the shoulders, he said: 'Madeline, you innocent, you shouldn't act like this! It's not right. Hell, why do you trust me? You've no idea how near I came to losing complete control of myself.'

Madeline wriggled free of his hands. 'All right,' she said, her voice cooler. 'You've made your point.' She turned and walked across the room for her coat. 'Thank you for a very pleasant and edifying evening, Mr. Vitale.'

Nicholas sighed and walked swiftly over to her, throwing her coat to one side and pulling her back against him. She felt his mouth move against her hair, and his breathing was uneven.

'Honey,' he groaned, 'I'm in no condition to hold you like this and talk normally. I want you, God, how I want you, but what I feel for you is not the same as I've felt for anyone else.' He swung her round to face him, and she saw his face was a little paler under his tan. 'Madeline, don't make me hate myself.'

Madeline slid her arms round his neck. 'Do you think I'm promiscuous?' she asked.

He buried his face in the softness of her hair. 'No, of course not. I knew you felt the same last night. I can't imagine why.'

Madeline shook her head. 'Nicholas, you're crazy. Besides, you'll probably regret all this tomorrow morning.'

He raised his head, and a half-smile touched his mouth. 'Honey, if I wanted to make love to you, could you refuse me?'

Madeline could not hide her embarrassment, but she bent her head in silent denial.

'So,' he said softly, 'I'm being very gallant, don't you think?' He pushed her away. 'Now, don't be foolish. I'll take you home.'

As Madeline retrieved her coat, Nicholas watched her. Never in his life had he met a woman who so violently disturbed his emotions. When he had invited her for dinner the previous evening he had been aware that something momentous was happening, but until now he had not realized just how powerful it was. Since Joanna's death he had known dozens of women, and was quite aware of the charms of money allied to good looks. Madeline, he knew, was different. He couldn't really understand how he knew that, but she was so far removed from any woman he had ever known that he was convinced he was right. He no longer felt the desire to be ruthless with her. She was almost an unknown quantity and he wanted to know her mind, her thoughts, as well as the delights of her curving body. This was entirely new to him and he felt an unreasonable jealousy for the unknown Joe.

Madeline pulled on her woollen coat and turned round. 'I'm ready,' she said quietly.

Nicholas noded and straightened up from the chair he had been leaning against. 'When do I see you again?' he murmured.

Madeline shrugged her slim shoulders. 'I don't know.'

Nicholas reached for his thick coat and put it on. 'Don't you?' he remarked softly.

Madeline looked helplessly at him. 'Don't tease me,' she murmured, and bent her head, the silky hair falling about her ears.

Nicholas buttoned his coat. He didn't trust himself to touch her again. He wasn't used to denying himself anything, and Madeline looked so appealing that he longed to keep her with him.

'Okay,' he said huskily. 'Tomorrow.'

Madeline looked up. 'But tomorrow ... Diana will think the worst.' She sighed. 'Ought I to leave her two nights running?'

Nicholas shrugged. 'Why not?' he frowned. 'Look, okay, bring her with you and I'll invite Maria to have a meal with us. How's that?'

He hated saying the words, but he had to see her tomorrow, somehow.

Madeline smiled. 'Thank you, darling,' she whispered, but he turned away. 'Can I ring you tomorrow to confirm it?'

Nicholas nodded and grimaced. 'Sure. Would it sound disgraceful, if I say I hope she refuses?' he grinned. 'Come on, let's go.'

CHAPTER FIVE

THE drive back to Evenwood Gardens was soon accomplished and Madeline felt regretful that the evening was over. She had enjoyed herself so much and parting from him now was like parting from part of herself.

'Where shall I ring you tomorrow?' she asked as they drew up outside the flats.

'It had better be at the factory. I shall be there most of the day. You know the number, don't you?'

'Yes. Will they put me through to you without any interrogation?'

Nicholas grinned. 'They will if I tell them to.' He sighed. 'I shall look forward to it. I only wish you hadn't a job to do. I guess I could take some time off if you were free.'

Madeline sighed too. 'Hmm, that would be nice. But I must go in now. It's getting so late. Thank you again, Nicholas.'

'Just make it Nick,' he said softly. A smile lit his eyes. 'As in the uncomplimentary title given to the devil. Quite appropriate, don't you think? After all, most people think I am quite amoral.'

'And are you?' she asked, her smile lighting the contours of her warm face.

He shrugged. 'You'll have to judge that for yourself,' he replied, and she slid out of the car chuckling.

He slammed the door behind her and leaned out of the window. 'Be good,' he murmured, and then set the car moving swiftly down the Gardens.

Diana was still awake, sitting up in bed reading when Madeline got in. It was only ten o'clock, but Diana looked angry.

'You've been sitting in that car for nearly ten minutes!' she said accusingly.

Madeline looked astonished. 'Have you been spying on me?'

Diana had the grace to look shamefaced. 'I heard the car arrive,' she retorted, in explanation. 'I looked out of the window to see who it was. I recognized the car as being a foreign one, so I presumed it was you.'

'I see.' Madeline took off her coat and hung it in the wardrobe. 'Tell me,' she said, 'did you like him?'

Diana made a moue with her lips. 'I didn't really have much chance to either like or dislike him,' she replied coldly. 'He seemed all right.'

Madeline's heart lifted a little. 'Diana,' she said tentatively, 'he has a daughter, slightly younger than you are. Would you like to have dinner with them tomorrow evening?'

Diana stared at her mother. 'On my own?'

'Of course not.' Madeline sighed. 'The four of us.'

Diana shrugged and did not answer for a moment. She was wondering whether or not she should agree. On the one hand, if she refused, Madeline would probably go and have dinner alone with him again, but alternatively, if she agreed to go they might think she was pleased with their association. And that certainly was not so.

Madeline undressed as she waited. She prayed Diana would agree. At least she would have the chance then of judging Nicholas for a longer period.

Diana was certainly having a battle within herself. At last she decided she would go after all. Her curiosity got the better of her. It would be something to tell the girls at school, having dinner with the owner of the new factory.

'All right,' she said, at last, albeit a little sullenly. 'But don't expect me to go into raptures over him. He's probably just amusing himself at our expense. How the other half lives!'

'I'm glad you've agreed to go,' said Madeline in a quiet voice. She did not trust herself to say any more. Diana was deliberately trying to antagonize her. Knowing her daughter as she did Madeline thought that Diana hoped to make trouble by going.

On Wednesday Madeline found it was almost impossible to concentrate on her work. The evening ahead loomed ominously. She was anxious about Diana. What if she behaved outrageously? She was so possessive. Never before had anyone shown this kind of interest in her mother.

Madeline took the opportunity to ring Nicholas during her morning coffee break. She rang him from the privacy of the canteen office, not wishing to start another argument with Adrian if he should find out.

Nicholas answered almost immediately, and it was good to hear his husky voice.

'Well,' he said, 'what's the verdict?'

'She says she'll come,' said Madeline swiftly, 'but I can't say I'm looking forward to it.'

'Why?' He sounded amused.

'You don't know Diana as I do. I'm afraid she might do something terrible and embarrass us all.'

He laughed, and Madeline bit her lip.

'Relax!' he exclaimed. 'She's only a child! I'm quite capable of handling children.'

'I wish I was as confident!' exclaimed Madeline with a sigh.

'You can be. I'll take care of Diana, should the need arise.'

'And if anything unforeseen happens, you won't take any notice of anything she says?'

'Of course not. Madeline, my love, I have a daughter of my own. Apart from which, I think I know a little more about the ways of the world, and men and woman in particular, than you do. Don't worry. I think it's almost impossible that anything she says should surprise me.'

Madeline pondered these words, long after she had rung off. She wondered if indeed he was right, and if so, what might he think when he knew her story? He thought she was young and innocent and delightful. Would he still think so when he heard the facts?

That evening they were dressed and ready to go when

Nicholas arrived to collect them at seven-fifteen. Madeline was wearing a short-skirted green jersey dress which suited her fair colouring, and Diana wore a strawberry pink linen shift. They both looked very attractive, and when the doorbell rang and Nicholas was admitted he did not fail to say so.

Diana looked sceptical, but she had to admit that Nicholas was a very attractive man. Dressed tonight in a light blue lounge suit, he looked suave and assured, and Madeline herself felt her head do its usual acrobatics at the sight of him.

They drove to the Stag and went straight up to Nicholas's suite. Diana had said very little on the journey; she had been too engrossed in absorbing the atmosphere around her and the hotel and its environs were as opulent as she had imagined. The suite lounge took her breath away, as it had done Madeline's, and at first she did not see the small dark girl who rose from the couch on which she had been lounging and came to greet them.

'Madeline, this is Maria,' said Nicholas, his fingers on Madeline's wrist. 'Maria, this is Mrs. Scott.'

Maria Vitale was vastly different from the irresponsible teenager Nicholas had described. Her hair was long and caught up in a loop of curls around her ears; she was wearing a trouser suit of dark blue velvet which bore the hallmark of expensive designing.

'How do you do?' she murmured, shaking hands with Madeline, her eyes warm and friendly.

'Hello, Maria,' said Madeline, smiling, and glanced at Nicholas. His eyes were enigmatic, but she felt sure he was amused by her astonished expression.

He turned and said: 'Diana, come and meet my daughter.'

Diana came forward reluctantly. Maria was not what she had expected either. She felt her own inadequacy become a hard core inside her and consequently her response was sullen. However, Maria showed no dismay and after shaking hands with Madeline's daughter she went to her father and said:

'Are we dining up here?'

Nicholas turned to Madeline. 'Do you want to dine downstairs?' he asked, and Madeline was conscious of Diana's annoyance that Nicholas should choose to consult her.

'I think it might best,' she replied softly, her eyes on his.

'All right. We'll have a drink first and go down later.' He walked across to get them all a drink. 'What would you like? The same as yesterday?'

Madeline nodded, and Nicholas said:

'How about you, Diana? Would you like an iced orange juice or a cordial?'

'I would like an orange and lemon,' said Maria, following him across the room. 'Would that suit you, Diana?'

Madeline crossed her fingers. But Diana merely replied:

'Thank you. I think I'd like that.'

The atmosphere was electric. Madeline was aware that it was probably partly in her own mind, but Diana's presence presented a kind of knife-edge drama. She supposed she was being ridiculous and wished she could be as relaxed as Nicholas and Maria.

They sat down with their drinks and Nicholas and Madeline lit cigarettes.

'Tell me,' said Maria, looking at Madeline, 'have you lived in Otterbury all your life?'

Madeline shook her head. 'No, I was born in London and I lived there until five years ago.'

'Oh, I see. I like London.' Maria sighed luxuriously. 'I've been over here about half a dozen times now and I think I should like to live in London, at least part of the time.'

'Then you'll have to marry an Englishman,' remarked Nicholas teasingly, but Maria shook her head.

'I think I'm going to marry an Italian,' she replied thoughtfully. 'They're awfully handsome, don't you think so, Mrs. Scott?'

Madeline felt the usual embarrassment at their out-spokenness. 'I don't really know a lot about Italians,' she replied quietly.

'I expect you soon will,' remarked Maria smilingly.

Madeline inclined her head, deciding not to comment, and Maria turned to Diana. 'What do you think?' she asked, trying to draw the other girl into their con-versation.

Diana shrugged indifferently. 'I don't think I want to get married,' she replied coldly. 'I think a career is more important than being some man's menial.'

Madeline felt sick with nerves. It seemed that Diana had decided to be difficult. She was about to make some reproving comment when Nicholas held up his hand and leaned forward in his chair:

'Some man's menial!' he smiled slowly. 'And what do you know about that, Diana?'

Diana shifted restlessly. 'I know that most men expect their wives to be continually at their beck and call,' she said sulkily.

'Do you have anyone in particular in mind?' Nicholas inquired sardonically. 'Most of the men of my acquaint-ance take an active part in the running of their homes and in the care of their children. There is a lot more to mar-riage than keeping house.'

Diana wrinkled her nose. She didn't want to know what his opinions might be. 'Well, anyway,' she said, 'I could think of better things to do than listening to some man boring me with his ideas.'

Madeline was horrified, but Nicholas merely raised his dark eyebrows and looked suitably chastened. Even so his eyes were twinkling and a smile tugged at the corners of his mouth, making Diana horribly aware that she was making a fool of herself. She looked at the faces of Mad-eline and Maria and while her mother still looked rather disturbed Maria was smiling, too. In consequence she suddenly hated all of them and pressed her lips tightly together.

The evening was a failure. Diana's attitude affected all

of them and Madeline for one was glad when dinner was over and they could leave. Both Nicholas and Maria had done their best to put Madeline at her ease, but she longed to get away.

Nicholas drove them home at nine-thirty. When they reached the block of flats, Nicholas turned in his seat, and said:

'You go on up, Diana, if you don't mind. I want a word with your mother.'

Diana got out of the car without a word, not bothering to thank him for the delicious dinner she had consumed, and after she had gone, Madeline looked ruefully at Nicholas.

'What a terrible evening it's been,' she said unhappily. 'I don't know what you must think of us.'

One hand cupping her head, Nicholas looked thoughtfully at her. 'What Diana does is not your concern,' he said. 'It's simply that she is frightened and confused by things she doesn't understand.' He sighed. 'I was not much help either, was I?'

She rested her head against his shoulder. 'She has no reason to feel like that. Surely she knows after all this time that I would never do anything to hurt her.'

Nicholas's lips caressed her cheek. 'I had better go,' he said with some reluctance. 'Can we see one another tomorrow?'

Madeline frowned. 'Could we leave it until the following day?' she asked, rather tremulously. 'That will give me time to try and make Diana understand.'

'All right. We will have dinner together, is that reasonable?'

Madeline slid out of the car and looked back at him. 'You do understand, don't you, Nicholas?' she said.

He gave an amused smile. 'I'm trying to,' he replied. Then he frowned. 'Just make sure you are ready when I arrive two days from now.' He gave her a whimsical look and then drove away down the road.

When Madeline got in Diana was already in bed and feigning sleep. Madeline decided there was little good to be achieved by rousing her and starting an argument, so she went to bed silently and did not even say goodnight.

In the morning, Diana went off to school with barely a word, and although Madeline ached inside she did not stop her. Why must Diana behave like this? After all, it was not as though anything definite had been decided. As far as Diana was aware, her mother and Nicholas Vitale were only friends and there was no cause for her antipathy except pure jealousy, of which she would have to be broken.

At school, Madeline worked automatically, her mind still active with the remembrance of the previous evening's dinner.

When she got home in the evening and she and Diana were having their evening meal, Diana said: 'Are you going out again this evening?'

Madeline looked up. 'No, I'm not. Why?' As yet she couldn't find it in her heart to be particularly understanding towards her daughter.

Diana shrugged her shoulders. 'I just wondered,' she said casually. 'Are you angry with me?'

Madeline gave her an old-fashioned look. 'Now why should you imagine that?' she inquired rather coldly.

Diana had the grace to look a little ashamed of herself. 'Well, I don't care anyway. I told you I didn't want to have dinner with them in the first place. They're not our type of people.'

Madeline gave her an exasperated stare. 'And who is our kind of people?' she asked angrily. 'I suppose you're going to bring Adrian's name into this again.'

Diana made a moue with her lips. 'Well, Adrian at least isn't amusing himself at our expense,' she retorted. 'You can't possibly think that Nicholas Vitale would seriously involve himself with you!'

'I think you're a very unkind and selfish girl,' said Madeline with difficulty. 'But don't imagine that anything you say will influence me in this. I'm quite old enough to look after my own affairs.'

'You're determined to make a fool of yourself!' exclaimed Diana.

Madeline clenched her fists. Her impulse was to slap Diana hard. She had no right to speak to her mother in that manner whatever her own feelings in the matter.

Instead, she rose from the table and walked into the bedroom, closing the door, and leaving Diana to her own devices. In truth, Diana did feel she had said too much now, but some devil inside her was driving her on.

The following evening as Madeline got ready to go out she wondered whether she was being rather foolhardy in risking her daughter's friendship for the sake of a man she had known less than a week. But when she went down to meet him all doubts sped away.

She was wearing a suit this evening, for it was warm and she required no coat. The slim-fitting outfit of bronze tweed looked well on her and tonight she had put her hair up in the French knot, and tendrils of amber curled in the nape of her neck.

Spring seemed to have arrived at last and the air was fresh and sweet. The sound of the river gurgling in the distance lulled her anxious nerves and she suddenly felt that what she was doing was right.

Nicholas helped her into the car and slid in beside her. His eyes appraised every detail of her appearance and then he said: 'Why have you put up your hair?' with a whimsical expression.

Madeline automatically ran a questing hand over her hair. 'Don't you like it? Does it look untidy?'

'I guess it's okay, it's simply that I like it loose. Don't ever have it cut, will you?'

Madeline smiled, relaxing. 'Not if you don't want me to,' she murmured, and his eyes caressed her before he put the car into motion and they purred down the Gardens.

They turned away from Otterbury tonight, towards Highnook, which was a village on the outskirts of the town. Beyond the perimeter of this section was a small hotel which Madeline had never even known existed. It was here that Nicholas took her, parking the car in the forecourt and consequently dwarfing the area.

Before they got out of the car, Nicholas turned towards her.

'I thought perhaps it might be better not to be alone,' he murmured softly. 'Do you mind?'

Madeline smiled. 'I don't mind as long as I'm with you,' she replied simply, and for a moment he pulled her to him and pressed his mouth to hers.

'I have some bad news,' he murmured slowly, his mouth against her ear.

Madeline's heart dropped to her feet and she felt the blood drain out of her face. 'What is it?' she asked, dreading his answer.

Nicholas cupped her face with his hand. 'I have to go back home tomorrow.'

'To Rome?' Madeline's voice was barely a whisper.

'I'm afraid so.' He kissed her eyes warmly. 'Will you miss me?'

Madeline sighed heavily. 'Don't be silly,' she murmured dejectedly. 'You know the answer to that.' She drew her face away from his hand abruptly.

He smiled. 'I know. But I'll only be gone for a few days.'

Madeline looked up at him in amazement. 'But I thought you meant for good.'

Nicholas chuckled. 'I know. I was just testing your reaction.'

Madeline shook her head. 'I think you're mean,' she said reproachfully.

'Do you?' He was smiling at her, and she cupped his face with both her hands. It was wonderful knowing she could be this intimate with him and she put her mouth lightly to his, tempting him but not satisfying his need. For a moment he let her have her way, and then his arms closed about her and forced her up against him. 'How am I going to go on like this?' he muttered at last, when they were both breathless and emotional.

Madeline shook her head and murmured: 'Are you sure you really want to go on seeing me? You're not just playing with me?'

Nicholas forced her head up and his eyes were brilliantly angry.

'I bet that little daughter of yours is responsible for that remark,' he muttered furiously.

'Yes, she was,' admitted Madeline wearily, taking his hand and holding it against the curve of her neck. As she did so, something hard dug into her fingers and she pulled his hand down again to examine the cause. It was an emerald-studded signet ring he wore on his little finger. An exquisite gold ring that must be worth a fortune.

'Do you like it?' he murmured, as she ran her fingers over the hard surface of the stones, and the initials engraved on the gold.

She smiled up at him. 'It's beautiful Did your wife give it to you?'

He shook his head. 'Joanna and I only knew one another for a few months before our wedding. I met her when I first went to the American branch of the company – her father was running the Detroit end at that time. I guess I was young and impressionable, and I certainly didn't realize that Joanna saw in me a chance to live an international social life. Anyway, when she became pregnant she wasn't at all pleased and she blamed me for ruining her life. Unfortunately the baby was premature, and while she was in the convalescent home she contracted a virus which left her in a very weakened condition.' He gave an involuntary lift of his shoulders. 'She died soon afterwards and naturally I blamed myself. But time has a way of healing all things, and Maria herself provided me with a reason for going on.'

'I'm sorry.' Madeline bit her lip.

Nicholas sighed. 'It was all a long time ago now,' he said. Then he drew the ring off his finger and taking Madeline's hand he withdrew her wedding ring and replaced it with the signet ring.

Madeline stared at him in surprise, and he said: 'You're the first woman to wear a ring of mine given in love. The rings Joanna wore were something else. I suppose you could say my father bought her for me. She came from an aristocratic Boston family.'

Madeline twisted the ring round her finger. 'But I couldn't possibly wear this, Nick,' she said.

'Why not?' he asked, gently removing the hairpins from her hair so that it began to tumble about her shoulders. 'There, that's better, I can run my fingers through it now.'

Madeline shivered in his arms and when at last he released her he said: 'I'll ring you on Monday, from Rome. I may have to go to Vilentia, too. Wherever I am, I'll get in touch with you. I leave in the morning and bearing in mind that I'll have most of Monday and Tuesday to work, I should get back on Wednesday or Thursday. Wear the ring while I'm away, please.'

Madeline hesitated. 'All right,' she whispered at last. 'If you want me to.'

Because of his impending departure, the remainder of the evening was bitter-sweet, and Madeline felt that the next few days would seem like years.

Nicholas was ever conscious of his own increasing attraction for Madeline and of how important she had become to him in such a short space of time. He wanted to tell her how he was feeling; beg her to go with him and marry him at once, but he decided against it. It was too soon. She might think he was spinning her a line. It would have to wait until he got back from Italy. He no longer felt any desire to go. His earlier, constant interest in the business had become of secondary importance now, compared to his feelings for Madeline. There was so much he wanted to do for her; so many places he wanted to show her. But first, he wanted to tell her he loved her, and hear that she felt the same.

He left her almost abruptly at the apartment, promising to ring as often as he could. He could only ring her at the school as she had no telephone, and it irked him to know he couldn't contact her direct.

Madeline felt near to tears as she watched the tail-lights of his car disappear on to the main road, but her fingers touched the ring and she no longer felt afraid.

During the days that followed, Madeline lived in a vacuum from which she emerged when he telephoned. As good as his word, he rang her on Monday afternoon. His voice was clear and seemed so distinct that she could hardly believe he was out of the country. He told her about his journey and his subsequent meeting with his manager in Rome. He told her he was missing her, but preferred not to say too much when there were so many miles between them.

Madeline hadn't mentioned anything to Diana about Nicholas going away, and if Diana had noticed the ring she certainly gave no sign. However, there was a large article in the paper about Nicholas's departure, and Madeline realized that Diana would not miss reading that.

On Saturday Adrian had come to the flat to ask whether their weekly dinner date was still on. Madeline was taken aback, but she said: 'Well, yes, if you like.'

Adrian frowned. 'Are you still seeing that damned Italian?'

As Madeline didn't know that he knew she was meeting Nicholas at all, she looked surprised, and he said hastily: 'Oh, I saw young Diana in town yesterday. She told me you were going out with Vitale.'

Madeline flushed. 'Hardly,' she murmured coolly. 'He's in Rome at the moment.'

Adrian was taken aback. 'In Rome? Has he returned so soon?'

'He has business there,' returned Madeline, looking down at her finger-nails to avoid his eyes.

'Very well.' Adrian turned to go. 'I'll be around at the usual time.'

'All right.' Madeline looked up. 'And Adrian ...' he halted, arrested by the tone of her voice. 'I don't want a repetition of this conversation, nor do I want a lecture. If we do go out, we avoid all discussion of – of Mr. Vitale.'

'Very well,' agreed Adrian, in an aloof tone. He was

slightly flushed himself and he obviously was struggling to say something. 'Is – is Diana taking this well?'

'Didn't she tell you?' Madeline's voice was icy.

'She didn't sound enthusiastic,' admitted Adrian awkwardly.

'She's not. But then she won't try to like Nick.'

'From what I gathered she likes him well enough,' remarked Adrian dryly. 'She simply objects to what she calls "your ridiculous attempts to cling to your youth".'

'What?' Madeline was astounded. How dare Diana discuss her mother with Adrian?

Adrian had the grace to look embarrassed. 'I . . . er . . . I naturally reproved her,' he said quickly.

Madeline frowned. 'Did you? Or did you encourage her? She's your ally, not mine.'

Adrian frowned and ran a finger round the inside of his collar. 'That was rather rude, Madeline.'

'But not uncalled for,' retorted Madeline hotly.

'She is your daughter, Madeline.'

'Do you think I'm allowed to forget that?' she cried in despair. 'Oh, go away, Adrian. Leave me alone, please.'

'Diana needs a father,' he said fiercely.

'But not anyone else but you,' said Madeline angrily.

'Diana thinks *I* am like Joe, her father!'

Madeline looked up at him, words trembling on her lips, words she knew she could not say.

'You've told me about him,' went on Adrian relentlessly. 'I can only assume that Diana is like you, though, because from what you have said, Joe was not a tempestuous character. Diana needs a guiding influence. The influence of a man, used to children.'

Madeline shook her head. 'Don't you ever give up, Adrian? I don't love you. I don't want to marry for anything else but love, can't you understand that?'

Adrian's face was drawn. 'Do you intend seeing Vitale again?'

'Yes, yes, I do!' Madeline almost shouted the words.

Adrian shook his head. 'You don't honestly take him seriously, do you? Why, he must meet hundreds of women during the course of his business and its accompanying pleasures. Have you any idea of the kind of life he leads, the women he's slept with?'

'Stop it!'

'I won't stop it! Somebody has got to talk some sense into you! Why, he's probably got some woman waiting for him back home at this moment! How do you know what he's doing?'

Madeline's fingers stung across his cheek before she could prevent herself, and Adrian stood, one hand to his cheek, positively astounded.

Madeline felt dreadful and sank down on to a chair. 'I'm sorry, Adrian,' she said wearily, 'but you asked for it.'

Adrian moved slowly to the door. 'Are you quite sure you want to see me tonight?' he asked.

'That rather depends on you, doesn't it?' she replied, sighing. 'What do you think?'

Adrian shrugged. 'I think perhaps you are right. You have your own life to lead. I won't obstruct you any further.'

Madeline knew what it had cost him to say that, and she managed a small smile. 'Oh, Adrian,' she said sadly, 'you're really too good for me.'

Adrian smiled too, his cheek still red from the touch of her fingers. 'I think perhaps you are right,' he replied softly, and walked out of the door.

After he had gone, Madeline resumed her work. There were so many obstacles really to her association with Nicholas. His money and position for a start. She would be just as willing to spend her life with him if he simply earned a weekly wage, but would anyone ever believe that? Then there was Diana. She was apparently very much against their involvement, although what Adrian had meant about her actually liking Nicholas, she could not imagine.

Madeline wondered whether Diana had read the morning newspapers and seen the announcement about Nicholas returning to Italy. She probably had, or if not someone else would have made it their business to inform her, particularly when she had mentioned earlier on that her mother knew Nicholas Vitale. Would she feel delighted at the news? Would she see this as a possible end to their association? Knowing Diana both possibilities were likely.

And then there was herself, her thoughts went on. Nicholas would have to know the truth about everything. She could not risk marrying him and have him find out from some other source. She would never know then whether he really objected or not. It was all very complicated and depressing and as she sat there alone with the prospect of a lonely week-end ahead, making everything appear so much blacker, she wished desperately that she was seeing Nicholas tonight. She could have gained confidence in his presence and the other problems would become of little account.

CHAPTER SIX

THE Saturday dinner was not a success. Adrian did his best, but Madeline knew that he was not happy. Diana seemed to have assumed an armed truce with her and outwardly everything seemed to be fine. The only black spot had been when a bouquet of red roses were delivered on Saturday morning and Diana realized that although Nicholas was away, he was not forgetting or forgotten.

But still Madeline was depressed and although the dinner at the Crown was quite delicious she ate very little. Half-way through dessert, a voice said brightly:

'Well, well. Surprise, surprise!' Madeline and Adrian both looked up in surprise at the accent, Madeline for a moment thinking it was Nicholas. But it was Harvey Cummings.

'Hello, Harvey,' she said, smiling, a little warmth lighting her face. At least this man was an associate of Nicholas's. She felt nearer to Nicholas somehow with Harvey by her side. After all, they were good friends. 'It's good to see you.'

Harvey recognized Adrian and nodded amiably, then he said: 'Look, I'm with Mary-Lee and Paul Lucas, why don't you join us? We were going on to a roadhouse near here, dancing. How about it?'

Madeline looked at Adrian. She knew he was not at all keen on dancing.

'Oh, I don't think so,' she murmured quietly. 'We usually go straight home after the meal.'

Adrian shrugged. 'Do you want to go dancing?' he asked, his eyes questioning. 'I suppose we could.'

Madeline shook her head. 'No, thanks all the same, Harvey.'

Harvey looked disgruntled. 'Oh, all right. Suit yourself, Sinclair.' He nodded to Adrian again and walked away, back to his friends.

'You could have gone,' remarked Adrian quietly. 'Come to think of it, I could have gone home, and you could have gone as Cummings' partner.'

Madeline's eyes narrowed. 'I do believe you're trying to get me interested in Harvey,' she accused him lightly. 'Do you think that one man is very much like another? I assure you it's not so. So there would be no safety in numbers.'

Adrian looked a little guilty and Madeline knew she had hit the nail on the head. How extraordinary that a placid man like Adrian should feel so strongly about something that he was willing to break the code of years to change things.

'Don't worry,' she said softly. 'It will probably come to nothing, as you say. If it does, you can have the last laugh and pick up the pieces.'

'I'm sorry,' said Adrian heavily. 'I must be very transparent.'

'To me you are,' she agreed, lifting her wine glass.

It was then that Adrian saw the emerald ring. His eyes became enormous and he said in astonishment: 'Where did you get that from, and where is your wedding ring?'

'Nick gave me it,' she said, knowing at once to what he was referring. 'Beautiful, isn't it?'

'Very beautiful,' he agreed, studying it. 'I should say it was practically priceless. That setting alone is the most beautiful and unique I have ever seen.'

Madeline felt her heart pounding. Nicholas had not said it was such a valuable thing. She had assumed it was expensive because of the emeralds, but that was all. Adrian of course, knew about such things. She found his eyes were on her now.

'I think perhaps I have been wrong,' he murmured, with a sigh. 'If Vitale has given you that ring, I hardly thinks he intends anything underhand.'

'What makes you say that?' she asked, her heart leaping a little.

'Because, my dear, it would have been quite simple for

97

him to obtain a ring and give it to you, one which would have satisfied you quite admirably, without giving you a ring that he probably values highly. I think, maybe, that Mr. Vitale is not as black as he is painted.'

Madeline smiled. 'I'm sure of it,' she murmured, and swallowed the remainder of her wine.

When they got back to the flat, Adrian came in as usual, and whether he and Diana were consciously aware of it, Madeline did not know, but they gave a good demonstration of how well they got along together, bringing back all Madeline's earlier depression.

The following week passed slowly, interspersed by Nicholas's telephone calls. Madeline's relationship with Diana improved, but Madeline knew that it was only a temporary thing. Nicholas's estimate of a few days seemed to have lengthened and although he rang she sensed a certain reserve about him. A week later on Sunday morning Madeline was having breakfast when the doorbell rang.

Diana was still in bed and Madeline herself wasn't even dressed. Trembling a little, she opened the door. She had really thought she might find Nicholas on the threshold, but instead there was Maria. Dressed today in a pillar box red trouser suit and a white straw boater, Maria looked exquisite.

'Hello,' she said, smiling. 'Can I come in?'

Madeline stepped back at once. 'Of course,' she said, but cold feelers of apprehension tinged her heart. Why had Maria come? It couldn't be a social call at this time in the morning.

Maria stepped inside and looked around her with pleasure. 'What a lovely room!' she said easily. 'It must be nice having a flat of your own. I think everyone deserves somewhere where they can completely be themselves.' She looked at Madeline. 'Nick asked me to come.'

Madeline's fingers tightened on the cord of her dressing-gown. 'Is he back in England?'

'No. He telephoned me, late last night.'

'I see.' Madeline tried not to be too eager.

'Yes.' Maria seated herself on the couch and said: 'I think he is feeling rather bad.'

A cold feeling gripped Madeline's stomach. 'Oh?' she said lightly. 'Why?'

Maria frowned. 'He expected to be back the middle of last week,' she replied. 'And I think he is afraid you will read a different explanation into it.'

Madeline hesitated. 'Do you mean he's worried about my reactions?'

Maria sighed. 'Yes, that's it exactly.'

Madeline felt relief flooding her being. She almost wanted to laugh, she felt suddenly so lighthearted. 'And that's why you're here?' she exclaimed.

Maria nodded. 'He wants to speak to you today. I don't think he likes the idea of always contacting you when you're in the school building.'

'Oh, I see.' Perhaps that accounted for the slight stiffness Madeline had noticed in Nicholas's voice.

'You're . . . you're very fond of my father, aren't you?' Maria said suddenly.

Madeline nodded. 'Do you mind?'

'No, not really, although I must admit that this is the first time he's ever been responsible to any woman for his actions.'

'You take it very calmly.'

'About Nick? I guess I do. I've not lived with him all these years without knowing him pretty thoroughly.' She looked diffident. 'He's a . . . wonderful person. I adore him. But I know that I don't fill the needs he has by any means. Everyone likes him, you know. He's so easy-going and amusing. Lots of women have wanted to marry him, rich and poor alike.'

'I'm sure you're right,' murmured Madeline softly. In her way, Maria was as isolated as Diana. But whereas Diana chose to try and destroy her mother's happiness, Maria wanted to help Nicholas, even if it was at her own expense.

Madeline carried her empty coffee cup through to the kitchen and Maria stretched lazily. She found she liked

Madeline Scott very much. She wasn't overly affectionate about Nick in that way some women adopt when they think they are firmly established in the favours of some man. And that Madeline was firmly established, Maria had no doubt. It was all quite new and incredible that Nick, who for so long had made playthings of members of her sex, should suddenly act in this wholly uncharacteristic way. She had known the minute he introduced Madeline to her that here was no passing phase. There had been something gentle and possessive about the way he had looked at Madeline and Maria had seen the first glimmerings of the shape of things to come. Her main worry had been that she might not like her, but she no longer was perturbed.

This attractive young woman had set all her fears at rest. She was sweet and kind and reassuring and apparently not a bit sure of Nick, whereas she had every reason to be. Maria had never known any woman but her grandmother intimately and she longed sometimes for someone to confide her hopes and fears in. She knew Madeline could be that woman. She was understanding and able to sit and listen.

Suddenly, another door opened and a pyjama-clad figure emerged, rumpling her dark hair. She stopped short at the sight of Maria, and a wary look invaded her eyes.

Maria smiled. She was always pleasant to people, no matter how rude she thought them, and she thought that Diana Scott was a spoilt brat.

'Hello,' she said easily. 'You must have slept well.'

Diana did not smile. 'Is your father here?' she asked bluntly.

Maria shook her head. 'No, I'm alone.'

'Good.' Diana reached for a comb and began combing her unruly hair.

Maria decided to ignore her rudeness. If Diana wanted to behave childishly she couldn't stop her. But couldn't she see how unpleasant she was making things for her mother; things which Madeline should be enjoying.

Madeline, hearing voices, came through from the kitchen. 'I've made some more coffee, Diana,' she said. 'Do you want some?'

'Please.' Diana dropped the comb and turned round. She took her cup and seated herself on the arm of one of the arm-chairs, her brooding eyes surveying the scene.

'Are you going out today, Diana?' asked Madeline, hoping Diana would act naturally and give up this stupid feuding.

'I'm going to the school with Jeff,' replied Diana shortly. 'The younger boys are practising cricket at the nets and he has to be there to supervise them.'

'Jeff,' Maria smiled. 'Is he your boy-friend, Diana?'

Diana looked scornful. 'Of course!' she said coldly. 'I don't want any breakfast, Mother. I'm going to get ready.'

Madeline looked anxiously at Maria as Diana put down her cup and flounced into the bedroom. There was certainly going to be no friendliness between them, owing to Diana's stubbornness.

'I'm sorry,' she said awkwardly. 'But Diana just won't accept the inevitable.'

Maria spread her hands expressively. 'But she will have to, won't she?' she murmured, watching Madeline intently. 'You realize that my father is serious about this?'

Madeline felt her cheeks flame. 'How can you say that?' she asked, her voice unsteady.

'I know him,' said Maria positively. 'Besides, you're the first woman he has ever introduced me to in such a manner.'

Madeline felt her apprehension disappear. Maria's words were balm after the last couple of days.

Diana emerged a little later in slacks and Madeline's anorak. She looked disdainfully at the others and said: 'It's ten-thirty. Jeff should be here soon. He's calling for me in his father's van.'

Sure enough, a few moments later there was a ring at the bell and Diana bounded to the door. She brought Jeff in for a moment, expecting to make Maria envious of her handsome boy-friend, but it didn't work out quite like that.

When he saw Maria he stared in astonishment, and Diana realized that she had made a mistake. But she had to go through with it.

'Maria,' she said, 'this is Jeff Emerson. Jeff, this is Maria Vitale.'

Jeff's eyes widened as he recognized the name at once. Maria's accent confirmed his suspicions.

'Hi, Jeff,' she said easily, looking very much at home on the couch.

'Hello,' he murmured, his eyes apparently glued to the girl in the red suit. She was so different from the girls he knew who favoured casual clothes, duffel coats and jeans. Maria had chic and her suit, although plain, was obviously expensive.

Diana's eyes flashed angrily as they continued to look at one another. Maria was amused. She had known how to handle boys from an early age and some of her charm was inherited from her father.

'Are you ready, Jeff?' asked Diana angrily. 'I'm waiting.'

'What?' Jeff swung round. For a moment he had forgotten Diana. 'Yes ... yes, I'm ready. Good-bye, Mrs. Scott. Good-bye, Maria.'

Maria nodded and Madeline thankfully closed the door after them. She wondered what Diana would say to Jeff when she got him alone. She had been furious as they went out of the room.

'Don't worry,' said Maria understandingly. 'She'll get over it. She probably thinks he's marvellous because he's so good-looking. I think he's a wolf. Harmless enough to me, but I'm not so sure about Diana.'

'Why are you immune?' asked Madeline, smiling in spite of herself.

'Oh, I've known dozens of men,' replied Maria lazily. Then she laughed. 'Listen to me! I sound like Mata Hari.'

'How did you get here anyway?' asked Madeline, lighting a cigarette.

'Harv brought me. You know, Harvey Cummings.'

'Oh, I see. And is he coming back for you?'

'Yes. He said he'd be back about eleven. He knows where to come. He likes you too, doesn't he? He said he saw you last night.'

'That's right. At the Crown Hotel. We were both dining there.'

Maria looked puzzled. 'Were you alone?'

Madeline flushed and shook her head. 'I was with a man called Adrian Sinclair. Your father knows him. He's a headmaster and my employer.'

'I see,' Maria studied the toes of her shoes. 'And Nick doesn't object? To you going out, I mean?'

Madeline shrugged. 'Why should he? Adrian is harmless enough.'

Maria smiled. 'It's okay. I'm only joking.'

Madeline decided to go and dress before Harvey arrived. She put on slacks and an overblouse and wound her hair up on top of her head. Then she and Maria sat together on the couch and talked.

Maria was easy to talk to. She told Madeline a lot more about Nick's home in Rome and his mother who lived there.

'Grandmother is a marvellous woman!' she said enthusiastically. 'She's only in her late fifties. She was eighteen when she had Nick. Isn't that wonderful! Grandfather fell in love with her on sight. They say thinks like that don't happen except in books, but I disagree. I think sometimes a person just knows when another person is right for them, don't you?'

Madeline had to agree. After all, hadn't she been attracted to Nick right from the very beginning?

'How about you, Maria?' she said. 'Have you no boyfriends?'

Maria shook her head. 'Boys bore me. I guess being with Nick such a lot spoils me for younger men. I like Harvey ... but he just considers me a precocious child. He likes me, I think, but he's in his thirties and I'm not sixteen yet.'

Madeline sighed. 'I think you're too young to care anyway,' she remarked. 'After all, with your opportunities, you're bound to meet lots of eligible young men and you'll forget all about Harvey Cummings.'

'I doubt it,' said Maria seriously, and then smiled. 'Let's talk about something else – Easter, for instance. We're going to Italy for Easter. Grandmother has a house in a place called Vilentia. It's about fifty miles south of Rome, a village on the Mediterranean coast. The house is divine, all flower-clustered balconies and terraces with fountains playing in the courtyard. Grandfather had the house built for her after the war. The village is just a collection of whitewashed dwellings, and the people are warm and friendly.'

'It sounds wonderful,' agreed Madeline, smiling.

'It is. Of course, I like the yacht just as much. My father called it the *Maria Christina* after me. My grandmother's name is Christina, too.'

'A yacht?' Madeline shook her head in bewilderment.

'Didn't you know?' Maria sighed. 'It's lying in the bay of Naples at the moment, I believe, but I expect Nick will go and bring it to Vilentia.' She laughed. 'Don't look so concerned! Naturally my father has all the attributes that money can buy.'

'It's rather frightening,' confessed Madeline. 'There's such an enormous gulf between us. I'm surprised he even looked in my direction.'

She was speaking half to herself, thoughts which were rampant in her mind, but Maria laid a hand on her arm, warmly.

'I think that's the reason why he did,' she murmured, 'if you won't think I'm speaking out of turn. Nick is so utterly sick of these society women with their penchant for handsome, moneyed men. They think appearances are everything and spend literally pounds or dollars, just as you like, a day on their faces and figures. You're not at all like them. You seem natural and unassuming, and you don't need expensive corseting to give you a slim figure, or loads of cosmetics to clear your complexion. A man wants a woman who looks as good in the morning when she gets up as she did the evening before when they were dining out.'

Madeline looked astonished. 'It's hardly believable that you're only fifteen!' she exclaimed. 'You seem to understand so many things.'

Maria smiled. 'As I said before, I've always had Nick to guide me. I don't think I could ever take people in our set on their face value alone, after the things Nick has experienced.'

Madeline reflected that Nick seemed to have made a better job of bringing up Maria, for all their rarefied atmosphere, than she had Diana.

There was suddenly a ring at the doorbell and Maria rose to her feet. 'That will be Harvey. I'll go.'

Harvey strolled in looking tall and familiar in light slacks and a sweater.

'Hi there!' he said, smiling. 'How's the gorgeous widow?'

Madeline managed to control her embarrassment and Maria giggled.

'Say, that was a nice brush-off you gave me last week,' he continued accusingly. 'There you were, with Nick hardly out of the country, eating dinner with that creep Sinclair.'

'Adrian is not a creep!' exclaimed Madeline indignantly. 'And Nick knows all about Adrian, although why I should explain my actions to you I can't imagine.'

'Ignore him,' advised Maria, and picked up her straw boater.

'I'm your guardian, Midge, while your dear papa is away,' he reminded her, 'and I'll have a bit more respect from you if you don't mind.'

'Don't call me Midge!' she exclaimed exasperatedly. 'The name is Maria. M.A.R.I.A.' She spelt it out for him.'

'Is that a fact?' exclaimed Harvey good-naturedly.

'Well, there's a little gem of wisdom I've learnt today!' He dodged Maria's playful punch and turned again to Madeline. 'Look, Madeline, how about you coming and having lunch with us today? You have to be there at two-thirty for Nick's call, so why not come now and be done with it?'

'Oh, yes, do come,' said Maria eagerly. 'Harv's right. Nick is telephoning at two-thirty.'

Madeline frowned. 'But what about Diana?' she exclaimed. 'No, really, thank you, I can't leave her to fend for herself.'

Maria grimaced. 'I would say bring her with you, but I doubt if she would come,' she said knowledgeably.

Madeline nodded. 'That's true. No, thank you all the same, but I'll come over after lunch. I can come on my scooter.'

Harvey shrugged. 'Okay, suit yourself. But I think you're crazy, turning down an invitation to lunch with me!'

Madeline laughed and they all moved to the door. 'I'll see you later,' she said. 'I'm sure Harvey will give you lunch, Maria.'

Maria grimaced again. 'I'm sure he will, except that Miss Sykes, my companion, will expect to be invited as chaperon. She's an English lady, who my father employed when I was just a child. I suppose that's why I can speak English so well. We use it a lot at home.'

'Ah, the good Miss Sykes!' exclaimed Harvey. 'A delightful person!'

Maria pushed him out of the door. 'She's all right, I suppose, when you consider she's a middle-aged spinster and rather old-fashioned.'

Madeline looked amused and Maria sighed. 'Aren't I unkind? Seriously, she's not so bad. Well, let's go, Harvey. See you later, Madeline. I may call you Madeline, mayn't I?'

'Of course,' Madeline nodded. After they had gone she closed the door and leant back against it weakly. Now she had time to wonder what on earth Nicholas wanted to speak to her about and she couldn't help but feel anxious.

As she prepared lunch she wished Diana had been more like Maria. They could have both gone for lunch at the Stag with Maria and Harvey and she had little doubt but that they would have enjoyed themselves. Harvey was very good company and she could understand how much Maria liked him, knowing that he was very close to Nick himself.

Diana came home in a bad humour. Jeff had spent the entire morning questioning her about Maria and she had naturally objected to it. Had Maria been a friend, Diana would probably have laughed it off, but Maria belonged to the 'enemy' and was therefore taboo.

She ate her lunch in silence and when Madeline said she was going over to the Stag to take a telephone call that afternoon, Diana raised no objections. Madeline wasn't sure whether she preferred the silent, moody Diana or the aggressive antagonist. Either way wasn't particularly pleasant.

She did not change to ride over to the Stag on her scooter and merely donned her sheepskin coat. It was fine, but a slightly overcast sky preluded rain later and the wind was still chilly.

The Stag was still full of lunchtime visitors and she felt rather conspicuous and unsophisticated in her slacks when she approached the reception desk. The reception clerk gave her a strange, aloof look and said:

'Yes, madam. Can I help you?'

Madeline nodded. 'Yes. Could you tell Miss Maria Vitale that I'm here? The name is Mrs. Scott.'

To say the clerk looked surprised was a gross understatement. The Vitales were his most influential guests and if this girl wanted to see Miss Vitale then she could not be exactly what she seemed.

'Certainly, madam,' he murmured politely now, and lifted the inter-communication telephone.

A few moments later a bell-boy escorted Madeline, via the lift, to Maria's suite. It was further along the same corridor as that accommodating Nicholas's suite and Maria herself opened the door.

Dismissing the boy with a casual smile, Maria drew Madeline into the room. As in Nicholas's suite the rooms were massive and opulently furnished and Madeline wondered how Maria could live in such surroundings without becoming a little prig. She realized anew that for all Nicholas's rather inconsequent manner at times he had given Maria a strong sense of values.

A woman rose from a low couch as they entered. Dressed in a tweed suit and thick stockings she could be none other than Maria's companion, Miss Sykes. Her rather sparse, mousy-coloured hair was fixed in a bun at the nape of her neck and Madeline mused that she was the living image of everyone's idea of a governess.

But she had a sweet and generous smile and Madeline took an immediate liking to her.

Maria introduced them and then looked at her watch, a slim platinum bracelet with a tiny watch face taking the place of one of the links.

'It's only two-fifteen,' she remarked, smiling. 'Sit down, Madeline. I've ordered coffee and we can have that while we wait for the call.'

Madeline was a bundle of nerves. She alternately wished the call was coming through and yet dreaded the outcome when it did so.

'I understand you work for a schoolmaster, is that right?' asked Miss Sykes, accepting one of Madeline's cigarettes, much to Madeline's surprise. Tobacco didn't quite fit in with the image, she thought half-amusedly to herself.

'Yes, that's right,' replied Madeline, glad of something to take her mind from the next few minutes. 'I'm Adrian Sinclair's secretary. He's the headmaster of one of the schools here in Otterbury.'

'I see,' Miss Sykes nodded. 'I used to be a secretary once. Not to a schoolteacher, though. My employer was a writer, John Brooks – have you heard of him?'

'Have I not?' exclaimed Madeline with interest. 'I've

read all his books. I think he's a fascinating writer.'

'Who's fascinating? Are you talking about me again?' A door had opened and Harvey strolled in and immediately the conversation became a light-hearted banter.

Madeline laughed and even Miss Sykes allowed herself a discreet chuckle. Coffee was brought in and they all had some, even Harvey, who remarked that something stronger would have been more to his liking.

At two-thirty, almost exactly, the telephone pealed shrilly.

Madeline felt her nerves jangle with the noise and Maria rose swiftly to her feet.

'There's an extension in my bedroom,' she said, indicating a door across the room. 'Would you like to take the call there, Madeline?'

Madeline blessed her understanding nature and rose too.

'Oh, yes, thank you,' she said eagerly, and Maria smiled as she lifted the receiver.

Madeline waited to make sure it was Nicholas calling and when Maria nodded her head, she walked quickly into the bedroom and closed the door. She had a hazy impression of rose-coloured carpet and drapes and a pure white satin bedspread, before she lifted the white receiver of the telephone.

She sank down on to a low basket chair and listened for her cue.

She heard Maria greet her father and then say: 'Madeline is waiting on the other phone. I'll let you speak to her right away.'

Nicholas's deep voice was music to Madeline's ears as Maria replaced her receiver and he said: 'Madeline, honey, is that you?'

'Yes, it's me,' she managed huskily. 'How are you, Nick?'

'In health or temper?' he asked a little dryly. 'Oh, I'm okay, I guess. Have you missed me?'

'That's a leading question,' she parried evasively.

'Well, I've sure missed you,' he muttered roughly. 'But

listen, honey. I can't get back before next Saturday.'

Madeline pressed a hand to her stomach. 'Oh, Nick . . .' she murmured, a little desperately.

'Don't you think I know how you feel?' he groaned. 'I want to come back right away, today even, but I can't. We're expecting some overseas visitors, buyers I should say, and the board seem to think they should take a more active interest in the deal. At any rate, I said I would stay for a few days at least. Can you understand?'

Madeline sighed. 'Darling, of course,' she murmured softly, and heard him catch his breath.

'I rang you today because I guessed you'd be expecting me back this weekend some time and I didn't want you to think I was in the country and not contacting you.' He chuckled. 'I guess I'll have to ring you every day for another week. Do you think you can stand it? or will I cause a riot?'

'I don't care,' she replied easily. 'I'd adore you to ring me whatever happens. It's wonderful speaking to you like this. I can almost imagine you're in the same room.'

'I wish I was,' he muttered intensely, and then sighed. 'I guess I'd better go out on the golf course today and get rid of some of this emotional turmoil . . .' He chuckled and she felt her stomach lurch.

'Who will you play golf with?' she asked swiftly.

'My brother-in-law,' he replied lazily. 'Don't worry, darling, there won't be any other women now.'

Madeline felt her hands grow clammy. His voice was so wonderfully warm and expressive and she knew in that moment that he meant what he said.

'I'm glad,' she managed a little tightly, wanting to cry because he was so far away and she so wanted to touch him; feel him close to her again.

'Are you?' he murmured. 'But surely you knew that already?'

'I think I did,' she admitted, her heart leaping. 'But I'll be glad when you're back.'

'So shall I! Now, about Saturday, could you come up to London and meet me when I land?

Madeline's fingers tightened round the receiver. 'Oh, yes,' she breathed expectantly.

'Good. I leave here late Saturday afternoon, so I guess it will be about seven when I arrive in London. Could you find out the exact time of arrival?'

'Of course. Will Maria be meeting you too?'

'God, no. I want you all to myself,' he muttered passionately. 'She already knows about this, so all you've got to do is get yourself to the airport in time to meet the plane – right?'

'Right,' she said, feeling lightheartedness stealing over her. In five days they would be together – well! six days anyway. It was wonderful.

'How have you been?' he asked suddenly. 'I've been so busy talking about other things I forgot the formalities.'

'Oh, I'm all right. I had dinner with Adrian again last night. Do you mind?'

'It's a bit late now to ask,' he remarked dryly, 'but no, I don't mind. I don't think I have anything to be jealous about there.'

'And Harvey? Would you be jealous about him?'

'Of course,' he muttered shortly. 'Hell, Madeline, what's Harvey been up to?'

'Nothing, darling. But he came up to Adrian and me last week and asked me to go dancing with him and the Lucases.'

'Is that right?' Nicholas sounded amused.

'What's amusing you?' she was curious.

'Simply that I asked Harv to keep an eye on you as well as Maria while I was away and he was probably trying to protect my interests by luring you away from Sinclair.'

'Oh!' Madeline felt reasonably pleased.

'Harvey knows what he can and can't do as far as you are concerned,' went on Nicholas softly.

'Does he? That sounds intriguing."

'Yes, but I don't intend going into that over the telephone. Not even when I know you are at the hotel. It has been terrible this past week telephoning you at the office. I always have the feeling that Sinclair is listening in.'

'Oh, Nick!'

'Well, anyway, this place has no appeal for me just now. My mother can't understand my restlessness to be back in England, or why I'm not going out as I usually do.'

'And how is your mother?'

'She's fine. She's naturally looking forward to visiting her relatives in America.'

Madeline was suddenly conscious that they had been talking for quite a while and she said: 'This call must be costing you the earth.'

He laughed. 'Not only in *lire, cara*. I'm convinced I'm losing weight by the minute.'

Madeline smiled at this. It was so wonderful to know that all her anxieties of the past week had been unnecessary.

'Well,' she murmured half-heartedly, not wanting to break contact with him. 'Saturday will soon be here. Look after yourself and – and be good.'

'Madeline, the only woman I want is a thousand miles away!' he groaned. 'I couldn't be anything else! Even I am unable to console myself on that score.'

'Good,' she whispered, her voice shaky. 'Good-bye, Nick.'

'G'bye, honey, till Saturday.'

Madeline replaced the receiver, and felt the hot tears flood her eyes, which was ridiculous considering she had nothing to cry about. Hastily she dried her eyes and stood up, looking at her reflection in the dressing-table mirrors. Fortunately the tears did not show and she hoped no one would notice anything amiss. She almost wished she could steal away without seeing anyone and relive every word he had said in private.

CHAPTER SEVEN

THE week that followed dragged by, each day seeming interminable to Madeline. The only bright spots were the telephone calls from Nicholas, but they were only short, and as she was at work she felt unable to express herself with any spontaneity. Nicholas was wrapped up in his work and was obviously finding it absorbing.

Diana, who had known that Nicholas had gone to Italy, couldn't understand why he hadn't returned, and she half began to think that he had indeed gone for good. Was it possible that his visit to England had only been a flying one? Surely it was possible that a man in his position should have to spend a great deal of time travelling around making certain that his subordinates were working smoothly.

She saw Jeff several times, but he talked about Maria Vitale and it was obvious that he hoped to meet her again. Diana got impatient when he said how attractive she was and refused to discuss her with him.

Madeline herself tried several times to tell Diana that she was going up to London on Saturday evening to meet Nicholas. Diana had a habit of changing the subject if she thought the conversation was veering into channels which she did not like and Madeline grew impatient with her.

Finally, at tea-time on the Friday evening, she said bluntly:

'I shall be out tomorrow evening.'

Diana shrugged. 'So shall I. I'm going to the club with Jeff.'

'I'm not going out with Adrian,' went on Madeline, 'so do you want to know where I'm going?'

For a moment Diana was motionless, and then she said coldly:

'I imagine, seeing that you are telling me with such

deliberate intention, that you must be meeting Nicholas Vitale. I wasn't to know he was back in the country.'

'He's not; at least not yet.'

Diana grimaced. 'Look, Mother, we'll have to agree to differ on this. I don't know what you imagine will come of it, but I'm sure if my father knew about it, he would turn in his grave.'

Wearily Madeline ran a hand over her hair.

'Joe was no prude, Diana. You are!'

'Prude? Me, a prude?' Diana was hurt and angry. Jeff had called her that only the previous evening when she had objected to the intensity of his kisses. 'Mother, I don't want you to get hurt, that's all.'

Madeline felt awful. That Diana should maintain an air of injured dignity was one thing, but for her to say that she was thinking of her mother's feelings was an entirely different thing.

'Darling, I won't get hurt!' she protested. 'Nick isn't like that. If only you would try to understand. Be sociable. Get to know him properly. You might even like him!'

Diana turned her face away, averting her eyes.

'Do you intend to go on with it, then?'

Madeline felt frustrated. 'Of course. Why not?'

'We've been so happy,' exclaimed Diana passionately, 'and now you want to spoil everything!'

'How? If I married Nick, how would that spoil everything?'

'Married? Oh, Mother, I'm sure marriage hasn't even entered his head! You're living on cloud number nine.'

'Diana, don't speak to me like that!'

'Why not? Uncle Adrian agrees with me. We can't both be wrong.'

'Diana! I wish you wouldn't discuss me with Adrian.'

'Oh, gosh, they're not our kind of people, are they? Apart from anything else. After all, you're getting a bit old to act like this. . . .'

'Old!' Madeline was speechless. Diana was always so

unfailingly disparaging about her age. She sighed heavily. It was obvious that Diana intended to play the ostrich and hope that if she did not look, the unpalatable things might resolve themselves in a way to suit her. It made Madeline wonder whether she was being the unreasonable one. There was so much to be said, and if Nick's life was virtually an open book, hers certainly was not!

Nicholas fastened his safety belt. They were coming in to land at London Airport. In a little while he would see Madeline again. He felt his pulses race at the thought of meeting her. It had been a long ten days and he had been impatient to get back to England after the first twenty-four hours. His mother, who was flying over the following Wednesday, had tried to persuade him to wait until then and keep her company, but he had made an excuse about business in England and refused her invitation. He had known she had felt hurt, but he was loath to tell her his real reasons for wanting to be back in case everything did not turn out as he hoped.

His mother had been urging him to get married again for years now, but she had in mind Sophia Ridolfi, the daughter of a distant cousin of his father's and an heiress into the bargain. Sophia was twenty-eight, small and delicately proportioned with a pale, interesting face. She doted on Maria and he was not being conceited when he reflected that Sophia would be only too eager to marry him. She had made it painfully obvious from the moment she was old enough to think about marriage. She had not cared that he had merely made use of her on occasions as his partner for certain business functions where a female companion of good background was essential, and she had always turned a blind eye to his indiscretions in other directions.

Nicholas realized now, that for the first time, he could not even tolerate the thought of marrying Sophia, or for that matter any other woman but Madeline. He had not really wanted to get married at all until now although he had often thought that another, younger woman would provide a companion and confidante for Maria. But Madeline's innocence and beguiling manner had completely enslaved him and in a way no woman had ever done. His marriage to Joanna had been an empty thing at best, arranged by their parents to satisfy the conventions. When she died he felt regret, but no more, as though at the passing of a friend. They had conformed to the expected pattern of matrimony and nothing more. Until now, Nicholas realized, he had never met a woman who he felt he wanted to protect, rather than take advantage of.

And yet, even so, he was unsure of his own attraction alone. Madeline was by no means a wealthy woman and the fact that he was virtually a millionaire must mean something to her. In what did his appeal lie; his money, or himself?

He stared moodily through the window of the aircraft, his sense of pleasure evaporating. Money was the very devil! He wondered if its advantages were greater than its disadvantages and then inwardly chided himself. Such thoughts were ludicrous. Of course the advantages were greater. He was thoroughly interested in the Corporation and without money there would be no Corporation. After all, his father had married his mother when she was only the penniless daughter of an Italian fisherman. He had not lost anything because of that. His mother had always been a wonderful wife to his father and when his father died she had been desolate. They had been so much in love and money had never entered into it.

The Boeing was coming in to land and seconds later they touched down. After running the length of the runway they taxied to a halt in the unloading bay. As Nicholas gathered together his belongings preparatory to disembarking he pondered about Madeline's first husband, wondering what he had been like. The thought had crossed his mind that there might never have been a 'Mr. Scott'. Used as he was to the wiles of women he wondered why her husband had died so young. Nine years ago, Madeline had only been twenty-four and even supposing her husband had been ten years older that would still only take him to the prime of his life. It was a thought worth considering.

He unfastened his safety belt and rose as the plane halted. He pulled on the fur-lined trench coat over his dark suit and walked to the rear of the plane with the other passengers. It had been freezing when he left Rome and he found the temperature several degrees lower in London when he stepped from the aircraft into the cold evening air.

The airport was a mass of lights in the swiftly falling gloom and he walked quickly towards the reception hall. He was well known at the airport and it only took a short while to clear his luggage which was being sent straight to the hotel in Otterbury. He carried only his briefcase with him.

The lounge was crowded and he wondered where he would find Madeline. There was no sign of her and it was already ten minutes to eight.

Frowning, he flicked his lighter to the end of his cigarette and hunching his shoulders he walked through to the bar. Pushing his way through the mob, he ordered a bourbon on the rocks and after fortifying himself with that he emerged from the bar again and wandered across the wide hallway, feeling strung up and intense. A feeling of anti-climax was taking hold of him.

Suddenly he heard a scurry of footsteps behind him and he swung round to find Madeline just about to catch his arm.

'Oh, Nick!' she exclaimed breathlessly, 'I was so afraid I would miss you. The bus got stuck in a traffic jam and consequently we only crawled along. I'm awfully sorry.'

She looked up at him apologetically, her expression one of relief and warmth at his presence and Nicholas felt his emotions stirring urgently.

'Why didn't you take a taxi?' he asked, forcing his voice to remain cool.

'I never thought of it,' she exclaimed frankly. 'Besides, a taxi would have been stuck, just the same as we were

. . .' Her voice trailed away. This was not how she had expected their reunion would be.

She sighed, and wished they could start all over again. She ought to have caught an earlier train, of course, but Diana had started an argument just as she was leaving and consequently she was late and missed the early train. But how could she explain that to Nicholas now when he looked as black as a thundercloud? He would think she was just making excuses.

'Well, let's take one right now,' suggested Nicholas at last, his voice still aloof and arrogant.

Madeline nodded, and turned to precede him from the building. Nicholas thought how lovely she was looking in her winter coat of dark green tweed with an edging of beaver lamb at the collar, cuffs, and hemline.

Most of the passengers from the earlier flights had departed now and they got a taxi quite easily. Nicholas gave the driver the address of a club in St. James's Street and then climbed in the back beside Madeline.

'We'll have dinner at my club, I think,' he remarked, as they moved away.

'Your club! I didn't realize you knew London so well. Or that London knew you for that matter.' She drew off her gloves nervously.

Nicholas shrugged. 'There are a lot of things you don't know about me,' he replied enigmatically.

Madeline digested this, and looked out of the cab window. She could not understand him in this mood. Had something happened to change things so drastically? She looked down at her fingers, studying the ring that sparkled so beautifully in its antique setting. She tried to think of something to say, anything to break this barrier he was raising between them for some reason. Nicholas sat in his corner, staring grimly out at the passing traffic, his lean fingers gripping the briefcase. She tried not to look at him, but it was difficult when she so wanted to just sit and stare at him, taking in every detail of his face.

Suddenly he turned and looked fully at her, the blue eyes narrowed. He saw the thick, silky hair swinging against her creamy cheeks, its brightness accentuated by the darkness of the loose coat. Her tawny eyes reflected the bewilderment she was feeling, but at his glance her lashes swept down, veiling her confusion.

'Madeline!' he muttered softly, and, unable to resist, he pulled her to him, gently at first and then more roughly as his mouth found the sweetness of her mouth, parting her lips, possessing her.

She struggled free of him at last, her cheeks flushed, her mouth bare of lipstick, her hair in disordered confusion about her vivid face.

'No!' she breathed, shakily, '*no!*'

Nicholas ran an unsteady hand over his hair. It was just as he remembered, only more so. She was everything he had ever imagined a woman being and he couldn't control his feelings as he used to be able to do.

'No what?' he asked, a little thickly.

Madeline pressed her hands to her flushed cheeks. 'Nick, what's wrong? Why have you changed?'

'Nothing's changed, honey. I guess I've been away too long.'

Madeline looked at him. 'That's not all, though, is it? I may not have known you long in terms of days, but I certainly know you better than that, I think.'

Nicholas shrugged and lay back in his seat. 'I guess we've been rushing things too much. . . .'

Madeline put a hand to her throat. 'Is that what you really think?' She bent her head, feeling suddenly desolate. 'Would you rather I went home—?'

Nicholas groaned and threw his briefcase on the floor of the cab and pulled her back into his arms.

'Oh, God, Madeline, why am I tormenting myself and you? You know I'm crazy about you . . . I want you, you know I do . . .'

She felt his mouth against the side of her neck, his lips warm and compelling, and she whispered: 'Don't tease me, please, Nick. If you want to end it, say so.'

'Tease you?' he murmured feverishly. 'Don't be foolish, honey. I love you, I need you, I want to marry you.'

His mouth sought hers, hard and passionate at first, softening into tenderness. Madeline felt as though she never wanted to be roused from this embrace. This was where she belonged. The spark that had been there right from their first meeting had ignited into a flame which only complete surrender to each other could assuage.

'You know so little about me,' she whispered, as his mouth moved to her cheek.

'Just say whether you love me,' he muttered, forcing her head back, his fingers encircling her throat.

'Of course I do,' she breathed, 'I think I did, right from the start. But there's something you've got to know, about Joe and Diana.'

Nicholas frowned and looked seriously into her face.

'What must I be told? That there was no such person as Joe?'

Madeline's eyes widened. 'Why do you say that? Don't you care if that's true?'

'Not particularly,' he muttered huskily.

'Well ... there was a person called Joe and he was my husband. He was a very kind person.'

'Kind?' Nicholas released her as they neared the centre of the city. 'That's a strange word to use to describe one's husband.'

'I know. But then ours was a strange relationship.'

Nicholas frowned. 'In what way? You had Diana.'

Madeline flushed. 'I know. Darling, I can't tell you in a taxi. Besides, we're nearly to St. James's Street.'

'Okay. Then you can tell me over dinner.' He smiled gently. 'God, have I missed you, honey!'

'I thought from your expression when I arrived that you wished you had never set eyes on me,' murmured Madeline, combing her hair into some semblance of order before alighting from the cab.

Nicholas sighed. 'I know. I'm sorry. I guess I just objected to being so completely enslaved by one woman. It's a new sensation for me.'

Madeline looked at him. 'Do you really mind?'

Nicholas gave her an amused look. 'Honey, you're

crazy! After all I've just said!'

'And it wasn't just said in the heat of the moment?' she asked, hardly daring to breathe.

Nicholas shook her head. 'No, not at all. I meant every word. I shan't let you get away, you know.' His voice was serious now, with an undercurrent of possessiveness that left her weak.

Madeline put her hand into his as she stepped out of the taxi and murmured: 'I don't want to get away,' in a husky voice.

Nicholas's club was an imposing place, quiet with the smooth efficiency of perfect service. He was greeted warmly and they were conducted to his table in the restaurant. As it was quite late Nicholas had waived the usual pre-dinner drinks and he ordered the meal immediately.

While they ate, Nicholas watched the play of emotions on Madeline's face. Something was troubling her and he wanted to tell her that whatever she had to tell him would make no difference to his feelings for her.

At last, he said: 'Come on, honey. Stop bottling it up. I want to hear about your marriage.'

The room was not full and they could talk in private without any fear of being overheard. The rest of the diners were mainly business men, engrossed in their own conversations, and those who were alone all had newspapers propped on the table in front of them.

'Well,' she began awkwardly, 'my parents were killed during the war and I was brought up by my grandmother. She was very good to me, but she was very strict. I had to be home every evening by nine-thirty and she always wanted to know where I was going and with whom.' She sighed and bent her head. 'I was, of course, rebellious. I began going around with a wild group of youngsters. I was at commercial college at the time. Grandmother had a house in Kensington and I used to spend every evening dancing or riding pillion on the motor-bikes owned by the boys in the gang.' She looked up. 'I suppose you can guess what happened.'

Nicholas lay back in his seat. He looked assured and handsome, and Madeline's heart turned over. What if he should hate her for what she had done?

'I guess you became pregnant,' he murmured shrewdly.

Madeline's face was crimson. She clenched her fists. 'Yes, you're right, of course,' she said, in a tight voice. 'But there was only one boy and then .. well ... only one time. The boy's name was Peter. He was tall and slim and handsome and I was flattered that he should choose me out of all the other girls. I didn't find out until later that he had had a bet with one of the other boys that ... oh, do I have to go into details?'

'No.' Nicholas shook his head.

'Thank you.' Madeline gripped her knife and fork tightly, the food on her plate of no interest to her. 'Anyway, I was frightened afterwards, but Peter just laughed and said I was a fool '

She didn't notice how Nicholas's eyes had narrowed, or how angry he was looking.

'He ... he crashed his motorbike a week later and was killed outright. He had always scorned a crash helmet and he didn't stand a chance. He hit a furniture wagon.' She shivered, remembering the terror she had experienced at the time; when she had found out she was pregnant and known that she had no one to turn to.

'When I found out I was going to have a baby I was desperate. I was sure if Grandmother got to know it would kill her. I went around in a daze for weeks, hardly aware of anything but the growing menace of being an unmarried mother and my child being illegitimate. Of course, I had no one to blame but myself. My greatest concern was for my grandmother The disgrace would break her heart.

'Joe was a professor at the college. He taught mathematics to the accountancy students and so on. I had known him vaguely for about a year, but only in a teacher-pupil capacity. He was a nice man, and I liked him. One day, he found me in the corridor. I had fainted and he took me to his office and gave me a drink to revive me. He was so gentle and understanding that I found myself telling him what was wrong and how foolish I had been. He didn't rant and rave at me that I was a stupid idiot. He merely dried my tears and told me not to worry. We'd work something out.

'It wasn't until later that he explained what he meant. He asked me to marry him.' She sighed. 'I was amazed, but he explained that his mother who had kept house for him had died recently and he was now alone. He said he needed someone to look after him and in return he would look after me. I was only seventeen and he was in his late forties at that time. I didn't have much choice really when I thought about Grandmother, and then of course there was the baby too. By marrying Joe I would evade the disgrace, so I agreed. Oh, I know it was a cowardly thing to do. Whatever I did seemed to be wrong at that time. I had behaved utterly foolishly and I had no excuse then. I can only say now that I never did anything to hurt Joe after our marriage and I think I made him happy.'

Nicholas lit a cigarette and inhaled deeply. 'You were very young,' he said quietly. 'Even today you appear somehow ingenuous. That was what I meant when I said you were naïve. Go on, tell me the rest.'

Madeline cleared her throat nervously. 'There's not much more to tell really. Diana knows nothing about it. She still believes Joe was her father. I haven't told her. She and Joe got along so well together and although Joe and I were never ... well ... quite as a normal couple should be we lived quite a happy life.

'I loved the baby and Joe was as proud and excited as any father could be.' She ran a tongue over her lips. 'It was when Diana was five years old that Joe developed cancer of the lung. To begin with I don't think we realized just how serious it was. They operated, of course, but gradually he got worse. He had had to give up his work, naturally, and I managed to get a job as secretary to the personnel manager of an engineering firm. With Joe's sickness benefit and my wage we managed to make ends meet. The house in Hounslow was his own and it wasn't far from my work. Diana had started school and it wasn't too difficult.' She felt a queer sensation talking about things like this. Until now, nobody had ever been told the full story.

'At last, Joe grew weaker and he was in constant pain. He practically lived on drugs and it was a blessed relief for him, I think, when he died. Diana was inconsolable. She couldn't believe she would never see him again. I must admit for a while I wondered whether our marriage had precipitated his condition. It seemed so wrong that I, who had acted so recklessly, should still be alive, when Joe, who had always been such a wonderful person, should be dead. The doctors were very kind. They gave me tonics and plenty of sound advice and eventually we managed to carry on normally. We had to sell the house and the proceeds helped us to pay the rent of a small flat I managed to get nearby.

'Well, as was to be expected, the money finally dwindled away. There was so much to be bought with so little and when I saw the advertisement for the post of secretary to Adrian I jumped at it. Living out of London was bound to be cheaper and my salary was to be higher, too. Adrian helped us to get the council flat and here we are. That's the story up to date.'

Madeline accepted the cigarette he offered her and looked thoughtfully into his face. She saw no sign of dissatisfaction there, only compassion.

'And do you intend Diana to know who her real father was?' he asked.

Madeline looked distressed. 'I really don't know. You see, Diana has such faith in her father's memory. I think she would hate to have that taken away. Even though Joe was only a father in name.'

Nicholas smiled. 'What better way could any father win a child's affection than by being there when she needed him? Joe was Diana's father! I think he must have been a pretty wonderful man.'

Madeline twisted his ring round her finger. 'Yes, he was.'

Nicholas's lean, brown hand closed over hers. 'Did you love him?' he asked, in a tense voice.

'Yes, I loved him,' said Madeline, looking fearlessly at him. 'But I was not in love with him!'

'Then why were there no more children?' Nicholas's eyes held hers

'Because . . . we. . . .' Madeline looked embarrassed. She had forgotten how direct Nicholas could be.

'Did he make love to you?' Nicholas's face was almost cruel as he forced her to answer his questions.

Madeline averted her eyes. 'No.' The word was forced from her lips. 'We had separate rooms '

'I see.' Nicholas released her fingers, reluctantly, as their coffee was brought to the table. After the waiter had gone, he said: 'So that is why you look so untouched. I don't believe you've ever known what love between a man and a woman really is.'

Madeline sighed. 'Probably not. But Joe was a very understanding person. I don't really think he wanted me in that way.'

'He must have been understanding,' muttered Nicholas dryly. 'Just don't expect the same treatment from me.' His eyes bored into hers.

Madeline smiled suddenly 'Oh, Nicholas, do you honestly think I want you to behave like that? I want you, too, remember? I want to share everything with you; be with you all the time. So much so that it hurts. . . .'

'Don't look at me like that,' he commanded violently, 'you've no idea what you are doing to me.'

'Maybe I do,' she murmured softly.

After dinner they went on to a night-club, a small, intimate spot where the lights were dim and the music was throbbingly primitive. They danced together on the pocket-sized dance-floor, their arms around one another, bodies close together, moving in unison. Nicholas's mouth moved restlessly over her neck and her face, unashamedly seeking her mouth again and again.

Madeline only knew that she loved this man as she had never thought it possible to love anyone and Nicholas himself had realized that all his life he had been searching for a woman like Madeline. Her complete candour commended itself to him far more than assumed artifice had ever done and he wanted to take care of her and make up to her for all the many pleasures she had missed. She hadn't had much of a life so far, and had paid dearly for the few moments of indiscretion in her youth. She had never known what it was to play.

Nicholas told Madeline that Harvey was bringing the car to pick them up at ten o'clock and she said:

'But that will be any minute now!'

'I know, but I thought I had better get you back in reasonable time for Diana's sake.'

Madeline smiled. 'That was thoughtful,' she murmured, pressing herself against him.

'Yes, it was, wasn't it?' he grimaced.

When they returned to their table, Nicholas was serious. 'Look,' he said carefully, 'we haven't got a lot of time and I want to get something settled. I don't care a jot about what happened in the past and I don't see any reason for you to tell Diana about her father. What I care about is you and me. I want to marry you, and soon. As soon as I can get a licence, if possible.'

'I want that, too,' she murmured softly. 'But Diana ...'

'Diana has got to be made to see reason. Good heavens, she's not really a child. She's almost an adult and should be treated as such. She can't go on ruling your actions in this way. You've got to be firm.'

'Diana still harbours thoughts of my marrying Adrian.'

'And would you have married Adrian, if I hadn't happened along?'

Madeline shook her head. 'No. I'm sure of that. My marriage to Joe was one thing; marriage with Adrian would be another. He would expect a wife in every sense of the word. Whatever he is like now, I'm quite aware of that. After all, he's a perfectly healthy and normal man. Why shouldn't he expect it?'

'Why indeed!' Nicholas nodded. 'But now that doesn't resolve things for us. Whatever Diana hopes about you and Adrian has to be ruled out once and for all. She has grown possessive and she possibly thinks that marriage for you with Adrian Sinclair would not take you away from her as she feels another, younger man might do. She also, I think, dreads the idea of you having other children.'

Madeline stubbed out the cigarette she had been smoking. 'I feel you're right,' she murmured slowly

'I'm sure I am,' he replied, swallowing the remainder of his drink. 'I've worked with a great many people over the years, men and women. There's always a logical explanation for everything.' He leant towards her. 'I want us to be married before Easter,' he murmured. 'We're going to Vilentia for Easter, to my mother's house there. Diana could come too, and be company for Maria. My mother would see that we were left alone. We might even leave them and collect the yacht. We could cruise down into the Adriatic; the weather will be wonderful. It always is. We would be completely isolated. You'll adore my country.' His eyes grew soft and caressing. 'The nights are long and languorous. I will teach you what it means to make love.' His voice was passionate. 'God, honey, don't make me wait any longer than that!'

Madeline felt her bones turn to water and she found herself clasping his fingers tightly. 'I'll come . . .' she whispered, but a voice broke into their conversation.

'Time to break it up, folks!' It was Harvey.

Nicholas flicked back his cuff and examined the gold watch on his wrist. 'You're five minutes early,' he remarked dryly

'Such a welcome!' Harvey was his usual amiable self. He subsided into the chair beside Madeline. 'Hi, honey, I guess you're having a good time.'

'Wonderful!' agreed Madeline fervently, smoothing her hair with a nervous hand. She looked at Nicholas. 'Are we leaving right away?'

'Hold on!' exclaimed Harvey reproachfully, before Nicholas could speak. 'Ain't yer gonna buy a guy a thirst-quencher?' He spoke in a Brooklyn accent and Nicholas grinned and signalled the waiter.

'How are things?' he asked when he had ordered three drinks.

Harvey stretched expansively. 'Well, now, they're just great. Did you have a good trip?'

'Pretty good,' nodded Nicholas lazily. 'By the way, meet the future Mrs. Nicholas Vitale'

Harvey's expression was incredulous. 'Is that a fact?' he exclaimed.

'It is. Madeline has agreed to marry me.'

Harvey shook his head, a grin appearing on his freckled face as the information sank in. 'Well, that's real nice. Congratulations!' He turned to Madeline. 'I won't congratulate you, honey. You don't know what you've landed yourself with!'

His good-humoured bantering set the seal on the rest of the evening. Madeline was relieved he seemed so pleased about it. It made up, somehow, for the inevitable argument which would ensure when she told Diana.

Nicholas drove the car back to Otterbury, with both Madeline and Harvey beside him on the wide front seat. Wedged between the two men, Madeline was only conscious of Nicholas beside her. They dropped Harvey at the Stag and drove on to Evenwood Gardens.

When the car halted, Nicholas pulled Madeline to him, his mouth feverishly seeking hers. They didn't want to leave each other and it was only Nicholas's iron self-control that prevented the inevitable.

'I love you,' he groaned. 'What time will I see you tomorrow?'

'I think you'd better come to the flat,' she murmured, running her fingers through the virile strength of his hair. 'I want to tell Diana about us, and it will give you both a chance to get to know one another.'

'Okay.' Nicholas released her. 'Go now, before I touch you again. I'll be round about two-thirty – is that all right?'

'Of course, darling.' She smiled. 'And thank you.'

For what?' He looked puzzled.

'For believing in me and for not being angry about – well, Joe and Diana's father.'

He looked tenderly at her. 'How could you imagine that I would feel badly about that?' he asked softly. 'Without your life being as sheltered as it has been, you wouldn't be the Madeline I love and adore. As it is, I shall be the first husband you've ever known. That means a great deal to me, honey.'

Madeline looked tremulously at him. 'Until tomorrow, then.'

He nodded, and she slipped out of the car without a backward glance.

CHAPTER EIGHT

As it turned out, Madeline was unable to tell Diana about Nicholas that night. Diana was already in bed when Madeline got in and was apparently asleep. She did not answer Madeline's tentative inquiry and Madeline could only assume she really had gone to sleep.

Madeline herself spent a restless night, tossing and turning, and awoke the following morning feeling as though she had never been to bed at all. Diana was sitting up when she opened her eyes, sipping some white liquid which looked like dissolved aspirin.

'Is something wrong?' asked Madeline, propping herself upon one elbow and looking puzzled.

Diana looked a little pale and Madeline was worried. It was not like Diana to be sick. And then she chided herself; everyone developed symptoms of some kind from time to time.

'I've been sick,' said Diana nasally, 'and I've got a splitting headache. I think I must have caught a chill.'

Madeline frowned and slid out of bed, pulling on her dressing gown and slippers. She padded round to Diana's bed and put her hand to her daughter's forehead. It did feel a bit hot, and she looked thoughtfully at her

'You'd better stay in bed then, darling,' she said, walking to the door. 'Would you like any breakfast? Some toast perhaps, and an egg.'

Diana shook her head, and swallowing the remainder of the aspirin, she subsided beneath the covers, looking wistful and withdrawn.

Madeline shrugged, and opened the door.

'I'd like a hot water bottle, please,' said Diana, suddenly. 'And perhaps one of those eggs whipped up with sugar and cream.'

Her mother looked doubtful. 'Do you think that's

wise? 'she asked. 'After all, if you've been sick. . . .'

'I'm sure I can manage that all right,' replied Diana swiftly

'All right.' Madeline went out, closing the door behind her. She went into the kitchen, put on the kettle and went back into the lounge to turn up the central heating.

After giving Diana the hot water bottle and the egg-whip, she made some toast and coffee for herself and had it in the lounge as she glanced at the morning papers. They were mainly full of scandal and after a brief skim through them she threw them to one side and wondered dully whether she ought to tell Diana about Nicholas at this time. After all, Diana was probably feeling pretty low to start with and that would possibly reduce her to tears. No, she could not do it. She realized it was partly cowardice that prevented her and that she was really putting off something which she didn't relish doing, but nevertheless, Diana was ill and she deserved some consideration.

That being so, she had better let Nicholas know, so that when he came round . . . or rather, if he came round, he wouldn't say something to upset her

She dressed in slacks and a sweater and making the excuse that she was going to see the caretaker about the rent, Madeline slipped out to the telephone.

She rang the Stag and was put through to his suite without much difficulty. Her name was now known to the management and the staff had been warned to treat her with the same deference as shown to the Vitales themselves.

It was ten-thirty, but when Nicholas answered his voice was drowsy and she realized he must still be in bed.

'Who's that?' he asked sleepily.

'It's me, Madeline.'

'Madeline?' His voice grew clearer. 'Madeline? What's wrong? Why are you ringing me, and so early, too?'

Madeline sighed. 'It's not early. I've been up for hours!

It's about Diana, Nick. She's not well. I think she has a chill or is sickening for something. She's in bed.'

Nicholas grunted. 'So?'

'Well . . . oh, Nick, I can't tell her about us today.' She frowned. Now they were out the words sounded so final. 'Darling, try and understand. . . .'

There was silence for a moment and then he said: 'So we don't tell her today But don't tell me not to come round, that's all.'

Madeline's fingers tightened round the telephone receiver. 'You are coming, then?'

'I am.' His voice brooked no argument. 'Listen, Madeline, you and I are going to be married come hell or high water. If not this week, then next week, and if not then the week after, understand?'

'Yes, Nick.'

'So. It will be well if Diana gets used to having me around right now.'

Madeline agreed. 'But please, don't feel angry about this.'

'I'm not angry.' But his tone was uncompromising.

'All right then, we'll see you this afternoon.'

'Check. See you about two.'

He rang off before she could reply and she replaced the receiver on the cradle with some trepidation. She wanted to see him very much, but she felt nervous about his attitude towards Diana.

Diana was fretful when she returned. She really did look distressed and Madeline got a sponge and bathed her face with cool water.

'Would you like anything else?' she asked, stroking back the hair from Diana's forehead.

'I think I'd like some lemon juice,' said Diana, nodding. 'Have you any lemons?'

'Yes. I'll make some.'

Madeline went through to the kitchen and put on the kettle again. She scalded the lemons with the hot water and within minutes had a jug of pure refreshing lemon juice. She cooled it, added ice and carried it through to

Diana. She poured some into a glass and helping Diana up on her pillows she gave the glass to her.

After Diana had drained it she said: 'Now, try and get some sleep. I'll come back in a little while and if you are no better I'll call Doctor Foulds.'

Diana shook her head. 'I don't need a doctor.' she said peevishly. 'I've only got a chill. I'll be okay tomorrow.'

Madeline frowned. 'Maybe. We'll see.'

When she looked in later, Diana had fallen asleep so Madeline just had a snack in lieu of lunch. She was too restless to eat anyway and was continually watching the clock. She worried alternately about Diana's condition and her proposed marriage to Nick. Easter was only four days away and the Vitales would be flying to Italy on Thursday at the very latest. So much was scheduled to take place by then. It was impossible, simply impossible!

Nicholas arrived soon after two. Diana was still asleep and Madeline let him in quietly. She still wore the green tapered slacks and a yellow over-blouse, her hair pinned up in the French knot. Nicholas seemed to fill the apartment, his tall broad frame dwarfing the generous proportions of the lounge. He removed his sheepskin coat to reveal dark slacks and a navy blue sweater, and looked darker himself in consequence. His hair which had grown a little while he was away now curled slightly at the ends and she found an almost sensual pleasure in just looking at him.

'Well?' he said, not touching her. 'How is Diana?'

'Not very well, I'm afraid,' replied Madeline, frowning. 'She had a temperature, I'm sure, and she has slept most of the day.'

'I see.' Nicholas pulled out the slim cigarette case. 'I'm sorry.'

Madeline indicated the couch and said: 'Won't you sit down?' Her voice sounded formal and a little stilted and with a raising of his eyebrows he concurred.

Madeline felt awkward. He seemed, somehow, to take

away all her natural assurance and she felt as nervous as a kitten. Sensing this, with the awareness of her he always felt, Nicholas flung down his cigarette case and linking his fingers round her wrist he said:

'What's worrying you, honey?'

Madeline tried unsuccessfully to release herself. 'What makes you think I'm worrying about anything?' she asked evasively.

'Don't fence with me,' he muttered, his eyes darker than she had ever seen them. 'Come here, damn you, I wasn't going to touch you, but I can see that I must. . . .'

He pulled her down on top of him, finding her mouth compulsively, and for a while there was silence in the apartment.

The stillness was broken by Diana's plaintive voice calling: 'Mum . . . are you there?'

Madeline got to her feet, buttoning her blouse, and smoothing her hair, while Nicholas reached lazily for his cigarettes and lit one. She entered Diana's bedroom and smiled.

'I'm here, darling. What do you want?'

'I want another drink,' said Diana, in an annoyed tone.

Madeline poured out another glass of lemon juice and was giving it to her when Nicholas came to the bedroom door and leant against the doorpost.

Diana's eyes widened incredulously and she almost choked on the lemon juice. Madeline wiped her chin with a tissue and said:

'We've got a visitor.'

'So I see,' said Diana coldly.

'I've been invited,' remarked Nicholas in just as insolent a tone. 'Have you any objections?'

Diana lay back on the pillows, and did not answer him.

'Sit with me for a while, Mother,' she pleaded, her eyes darting at Nicholas's face. 'I feel lonely.'

'Then join us in the lounge,' said Nicholas bleakly.

Diana looked hurt. 'I'm not very well.'

'Aren't you?' Nicholas looked sceptical. 'Have you seen a doctor?'

'No,' Madeline answered.

'I've told you!' exclaimed Diana angrily. 'I don't need a doctor.'

'Do you treat yourself?' asked Nicholas sarcastically. 'I think you ought to see a doctor.'

Madeline looked anxious. 'Do you really?'

'No, not really,' retorted Nicholas. 'I simply want Diana to have the best of attention.' He was well aware that Diana was casting absolutely killing glances in his direction.

'Well, will you phone him? Dr. Foulds. The number is in the book.'

'Sure.' Nicholas straightened up, ignoring Diana. 'Where's the nearest phone booth?'

Madeline gave him directions and with a sardonic salute to Diana, Nicholas left the apartment.

After he had gone, Diana looked furiously at her mother. 'You let him do that on purpose. You're both hateful!'

Madeline gasped, 'But why? We only want you to feel better as soon as possible.'

'Why? So that you can feel free to go out whenever you like?'

'That was uncalled-for, Diana.'

'Was it?' Diana was mutinous. 'All right! Have the doctor! See if I care!'

Dr. Foulds was an elderly man, but he came at once. After examining Diana he came back into the lounge, and folded his stethoscope back into his bag.

'Frankly, Mrs. Scott,' he said deliberately, 'there's nothing much wrong with Diana that I can see. Apart from a little nasal congestion which may be due to a slight cold in the head.'

'But her temperature?'

'. . . is quite normal,' finished the doctor, smiling benevolently. 'I think your daughter is swinging the lead.

Mrs. Scott. Doesn't she want to go to school tomorrow?'

Madeline hardly dared look at Nicholas. 'But she was sick, doctor. . . .'

'Did you actually see her, being sick I mean?'

'Why . . . no.'

'Exactly. As I thought, my dear. Young Diana will have to have a good talking to, calling a hard-working doctor out for nothing.'

'I'm awfully sorry.' Madeline felt guilty.

'That's all right. As it happens I've had quite an easy weekend. Tell that girl of yours to get herself to school and stop havering, or I'll put her over my knee. She's not too big yet, you know!'

'Thank you, doctor.' Madeline ushered him to the door. She felt awful, both about Nicholas and the doctor now.

After he had gone she turned back into the lounge to find Nicholas standing staring out of the window. He swung round and said:

'You realize this whole performance was for our benefit?'

Madeline rubbed her elbows with the palms of her hands, arms crossed, feeling unable to answer him. She knew he must be right and yet she still didn't want to accept it.

Nicholas moved restlessly. 'God, she must think we're complete idiots! Well, she's not going to get away with it!'

Madeline looked up at him. 'With what?'

'This idea that if she feels like staging an illness all actions on our part will be suspended, possibly even cancelled.'

'What are you going to do?'

'Tell her the truth, now!' Nicholas thrust his hands into his trousers pockets. 'She obviously realized that you might conceivably be harbouring something more distasteful to her than a mere casual affair.'

Madeline caught his arm. 'Nick, I'm sure you're right,

but we can't go into all that now. Not this minute.'

'Why?' His voice was cold.

Madeline shrugged, unable to find words. 'Oh, I suppose I want everything to be right between us, and now it's going to be a slanging match and goodness knows how long the enmity will last.'

Nicholas scowled. 'Madeline, you're afraid to tell her!' he muttered accusingly. 'This is Sunday, remember. My mother arrives on Wednesday and we leave for Vilentia on Thursday. How much longer do you expect to delay the evil day?'

'I don't know ....' Madeline turned away. 'It's so sudden.'

'Sudden? Sudden? Madeline, do you want me to wait indefinitely until you pluck up enough courage to face your own daughter with something that ought to cause you great happiness, not discontent?'

'No, I don't want to wait. I just don't want to break Diana's heart. ...'

Nicholas grunted. 'I fancy your daughter's heart is a little harder to break than others I could mention. Are you going to tell her now?' His voice was hard.

'I ... I ... Nick, please. ...'

Nicholas reached for his coat abruptly, his face enigmatic, although his eyes blazed with anger.

'Wh ... where are you going?' Her heart was in her mouth.

'Back to the hotel,' muttered Nicholas, walking to the door.

'Oh, no! Nick, don't go like this ...' she began desperately.

Nicholas ignored her pleas and opened the door and went out closing it behind him before she could stop him. This was a painful experience for him too. No woman had ever openly defied him before and it was all the more humiliating to know that for all her indecision and stumbling cowardice he still wanted her, so much so that had he stayed there he would have relented and agreed to a postponement of their marriage for a long as she wanted it.

Madeline, left alone, sank down bitterly on the couch, hot tears overflowing her eyes and streaming uninhibitedly down her cheeks. The full impact of what she had done was washing over her and it horrified her.

CHAPTER NINE

NICHOLAS drove straight back to the Stag. He was in a violent temper and barely answered the desk clerk when he greeted him. Ignoring the lift, he mounted the stairs to Maria's suite impatiently and flung open the doors, walking arrogantly into the room.

Maria was alone, stretched out on a couch reading a magazine, and eating her way through a box of chocolates. She smiled lazily up at him as he came in, wondering what on earth had brought him back so soon and in such a flaming mood. His face was as black as a thunder cloud and she had to discipline herself not to question what was wrong. She had learned many years ago not to ask those sort of questions unless she was prepared for a tirade in place of an answer.

'Hello!' she greeted him cheerfully in English. 'This is a surprise.' They often used English when they were alone as Nicholas had spent so much time in the States that it was his second language.

Nicholas flung himself into a low armchair, loosening his coat. 'Get me a drink,' he said abruptly. 'You know what I like.'

'And how you like it,' remarked Maria lightly, and slid nimbly off the couch. She was dressed in skin-tight red trews and a sleeveless sweater, her hair caught up in a ponytail. She looked fresh and uncomplicated to Nicholas's slightly jaded eyes. Why couldn't Diana Scott have been a normal well-balanced child?

'Here you are, darling,' said Maria, handing him a glass of cool liquid. She frowned. 'Do you feel all right?'

Nicholas shook his head. 'No, I feel smashed!' he muttered with a deepening of his scowl, and Maria subsided on to the couch again, feeling suitably abashed. She retrieved her magazine and Nicholas stared moodily across at her. 'Where's Miss Sykes?'

'In her room – why? Do you want to see her?'

'No,' grunted Nicholas. 'What have you been doing, apart from stuffing yourself with chocolates?'

'Nothing much. We went walking, as you know, this morning and had coffee in a genuine English tea-room. At least, that was what it called itself, but I think it was a pretty low place. Very exciting.' She smiled.

Nicholas was bored. He rose to his feet. The tortuous feeling in his bones was exasperating to say the least and he knew he wouldn't sleep well tonight.

He took off his overcoat and flung it over a chair, walking restlessly about the room. He looked like a magnificent, caged animal and Maria enjoyed watching him. She was very proud of her father. But she knew that something was seriously wrong and she said:

'Don't prowl, darling. You make me nervous.'

Nicholas ignored her remark and continued his pacing. Pouring himself another drink, he said: 'Do you want to go for a drive?'

'I . . . I guess we could. Are you sure it's me you want to take?'

'Quite sure,' he muttered savagely.

Maria shrugged and rose to her feet. 'Don't snap my head off. I only asked a simple question. Judging from your expression I'd say I was the last person you wanted to be with.'

Nicholas's scowl deepened. 'What the hell do you mean by that remark?'

'Well, there are female companions . . . and female companions,' she replied shrewdly. 'Right now, I'd say you needed something different to the companionship of a daughter.'

'The devil you would,' he muttered. 'Well, you're mistaken.'

'What about Madeline, then?' asked Maria, unable to prevent the words.

'Forget about Madeline,' he advised coldly. 'Are you going to change?'

'Of course. Don't be so grumpy. This is Maria . . . remember?'

'Sure.' Nicholas's eyes softened for a moment. 'All right, minx. Don't keep me waiting.'

He smacked her behind as she passed him and she smiled gaily up at him. Whatever was wrong, she was not going to be told at the moment.

She dressed in white trousers of heavy silk jersey which had a matching jacket piped with scarlet. White pumps completed the ensemble and she looked more like an eighteen-year-old than the fifteen-year-old she was. Nicholas felt a sense of pride as she joined him. She was so poised and assured, and very much like him, although just now he didn't feel either spoiled or assured.

The red Sheridan waited in the parking lot and Maria slid in feeling quite pleased about the unexpected outing. Since her arrival in England her father had not found much time for her and now she felt justifiably pleased that they were together.

The market place in Otterbury was busy this Sunday afternoon. Groups of young people stood around talking and laughing together and Maria envied them their complete naturalness. At home in Italy she had had loads of friends and had spent most weekends on the Lake, sailing and swimming. She missed the free and easy companionship of boys and girls of her own age, not knowing any young people in Otterbury. Still, she consoled herself, she was here with Nick and Harvey, and that made up for quite a lot.

Suddenly she sat forward in her seat. 'There's that boy that Diana Scott is friendly with. He looks as though he's waiting for somebody. Do you think it might be Diana?'

'Very likely,' remarked Nicholas dryly. 'However, if he is he will be having a long wait in vain. She won't be coming. She's in bed.' He sounded sardonic and Maria glanced at him for a moment.

'Is she ill?'

'So she says,' replied Nicholas, his fingers tightening on the wheel.

'Then don't you think we ought to stop and tell him?' asked Maria, at once. 'After all, he looks fed up already. Perhaps he's been waiting quite a while.'

Nicholas shrugged. He had no particular desire to speak to someone who knew the Scotts well, but it seemed he had no option without having to answer a lot of pertinent questions from his daughter.

He swung the car purposefully round the Square and drove back to where Jeff was standing.

Maria wound down her window. 'Say!' she said, attracting Jeff's attention at once. The massive Sheridan automobiles always caused a stir in Otterbury. 'Are you waiting for Diana?'

Jeff walked across to them, looking surprised but not displeased, and Maria said swiftly: 'Couldn't we ask him to come with us?' in a low voice to her father.

'I guess so.' Nicholas sounded non-committal.

'Well, it will be great having someone young to speak to for a change.'

'Thank you.' Nicholas gave her a sidelong glance and she giggled.

'You know I don't mean that in a derogatory fashion,' she whispered, as Jeff reached the car.

'Yes,' he said, leaning on the window, 'I'm waiting for Diana.' His eyes appraised the lovely picture Maria made sitting in the luxurious car and he suddenly decided he didn't care that Diana wasn't coming any more.

'She's ill in bed,' said Maria, her eyes sparkling. 'She won't be coming. Are you at a loose end now?'

Jeffs eyes narrowed. 'I suppose so.'

'Then how about coming with us? I don't exactly know where we're going but it will be better than hanging around here.'

Jeff's face was flushed. 'But I mean. . . .' He glanced at Nicholas. 'Doesn't your ... er ... friend ... mind?'

Maria laughed merrily. 'This is my father,' she said, by way of an introduction. 'He doesn't mind. Get in.'

She slid along the front seat so that Jeff could get in beside them and Nicholas found himself remembering that only the previous evening Madeline had occupied that same position, close beside him.

His anger surfaced again and he set the car moving violently, startling a crowd of teenagers who were admiring the car close by.

Nicholas slept badly as he had expected he would. He tossed restlessly in the big bed, getting up twice to take some aspirin without any result. He got up at seven in a foul mood, his head aching abominably.

He wasted time, reading newspapers and generally moping about, and did not put in an appearance at the factory until eleven o'clock. He strode through the glass doors of the building and was hailed by a receptionist.

'Mr. Vitale! There's a young lady waiting to see you, sir. She's been waiting since ten o'clock. She said it was a personal matter, so I put her in the interview room.'

Nicholas's pulse increased. Madeline! He felt the blood pounding in his ears. Who else could it be, after all?

He crossed the wide hallway and thrust open the door of the interview room. As he did so, a girl rose from the chair by the desk. It was Diana Scott!

For a few seconds his disappointment stunned him. He couldn't believe he was seeing aright and it was an effort to pull himself together and close the door. His eyes were as cold as a glacier as they looked at the girl and Diana clenched her hands in her lap.

'Good morning, Mr. Vitale,' she said uneasily, subsiding into the chair again.

Nicholas did not immediately reply. He walked slowly round the desk and seated himself opposite her in the low armchair.

'Why are you here?' he asked bluntly.

Diana flushed. 'I'll tell you, Mr. Vitale. I want you to stop seeing my mother.' She cleared her throat. 'For good.'

Nicholas's expression was frightening.

'Are you serious?' he demanded savagely.

Diana swallowed hard. 'Of course I am. Look . . . we

were happy till you cane along, disrupting our lives, turning my mother against me.'

'You have turned your mother against you, not me,' he muttered, 'although, by God, I can't see how you can say that after the way she thinks of you before her own happiness.'

'Well, she's never acted in this way before. She treats me as though I were an encumbrance. . . .'

'Rubbish!'

'It's true,' Diana sneered. 'She thinks that because you're paying her a lot of attention you're serious about her.'

'I don't know how you dare come here and discuss your own mother in this outrageous fashion,' he exclaimed angrily, standing up. 'Who the hell do you think you are, anyway?'

Diana compressed her lips at this outburst. Then she went on scornfully: 'I love my mother. I don't want her to be hurt. Uncle Adrian wants to marry her. Do you think he'll want her . . . after you?'

'Shut your mouth!' Nicholas commanded furiously. 'How dare you say you love your mother? You love only one person – Diana Scott. You're terrified in case your mother does marry me. You're not concerned whether she gets hurt or not. All you're really worried about is whether you're going to have your nose put out of joint. After all, we might have other children, mightn't we?'

Diana's face whitened as though he had struck her and she rose unsteadily to her feet.

'I think the whole affair is disgusting,' she exclaimed wildly. 'How can you say things like that to me?'

'Because they're true. Don't hedge with me, Diana, it won't work. I can see through you like I can see through glass. You're patently transparent.' He was in no mood to spare her feelings and he rested his hands on the desk, facing her. 'What's – disgusting about marriage, anyway?'

' N. . . nothing. But you aren't like Daddy or Uncle Adrian. You're . . . oh . . . you're horrible!'

Nicholas sighed wearily, controlling his temper with an effort.

'Tell me why?' he said quietly. 'And if you can't, I'll tell you.'

Diana twisted her fingers together. 'What do you mean?'

'I mean that until these last four weeks you never even thought of your mother as still being an attractive young woman. Even now, you don't accept it. You think I'm horrible because I don't conform to your petty ideas of what a man who marries your mother should be. As I said before, Diana, you're concerned for yourself. If you really thought a lot of your mother you might stop to consider that she might have found someone who could make her happy . . . really happy.'

'She'll never be happy with you!' cried Diana, her breast heaving.

Nicholas was unable to take any more of this. 'Get out!' he muttered, 'before I lose my temper altogether. Out!'

Diana rose and backed to the door. 'You're hateful!' she exclaimed, her voice unsteady. She went out swiftly banging the door.

After she had gone, Nicholas sank down on to the side of the desk, lighting a cigarette with rather unsteady fingers.

What a hell of a thing to happen! He wondered how many men had been confronted like that by the daughters of their prospective wives. He shook his head wearily. Still, as things stood he could hardly call Madeline his prospective wife. After yesterday they were hardly even friends.

He sighed. He was utterly sickened by the whole affair. He wanted to marry Madeline more than anything else in the world, of that he was certain, but how could he accept a marriage where Diana was treated as being of greater importance than he was? Maybe his was a strict notion, but he couldn't accept it any other way.

CHAPTER TEN

MADELINE found the days following Nicholas's abrupt departure from the flat almost more than she could bear. She did her work automatically, inwardly crying for the love she had lost. Diana had remained in bed all day Sunday, but Madeline had not had the stomach to tell her what the doctor had said. She saw the self-satisfied smile on Diana's face when she heard that Nicholas had left and had been too hurt to say any more.

On Monday Diana went to school as usual and she began treating Madeline with her old affection, but although Madeline submitted in silence she did not respond. She could not. She felt mentally exhausted and dreaded going to work to face Adrian.

However, after inquiring whether Nicholas got back on Saturday Adrian did not make any comment and Madeline was thankful. She did not know what she could reply.

She half-hoped that Nicholas might telephone, but she was doomed to disappointment. She felt helpless. Surely he didn't intend their affair to end; just like that. Of course, Adrian had warned her that he was not the type to tangle with, but that was not why he had stormed out of the flat. He had despised her for her indecision, her cowardice over Diana, and most of all her refusal to put him first.

Diana stormed home in a rage on Monday evening, her earlier solicitude forgotten. Madeline asked her wearily what was wrong and Diana swung round angrily.

'Your precious boy-friend's daughter was out with Jeff yesterday,' she flared.

'Out with Jeff? How did that come about? And anyway, how do you know? You were in bed.'

Diana flushed. 'Jeff told me. I met him at lunchtime and he couldn't wait to blurt it out. He was waiting for

146

me in the market yesterday when Maria and her father came by in that jazzy car of theirs. Maria told him that I was ill and wouldn't be coming and kindly suggested that he should go with them! They went to London, spent some time looking around and then Mr. Vitale bought them dinner in a plushy grillroom in the West End. You should have heard Jeff! He was positively gloating over it. He says Maria is terrific and has got what it takes, etc., etc.,' Diana scowled.

She couldn't very well go on to tell her mother that Jeff was getting a little too ardent in his lovemaking and was continually asking her to relax and stop being so frigid when he tried to make love to her. He had as good as told her that Maria was not like that and that had they been alone he could have really enjoyed himself. He had said Diana was prudish and ought to wake up to life and stop living in a dream world. Diana, young and confused, unable to tell anyone about it, was finding life very complicated at the moment.

'Well, I shouldn't worry over that,' remarked Madeline cynically. 'I hardly think that Maria will have a great deal to do with Jeff Emerson; not if her father has anything to do with it anyway.'

Diana felt her cheeks burning, remembrance of the morning's interview with Nicholas Vitale fresh in her mind. She glanced surreptitiously at her mother. Apparently he hadn't rung her. She had half-expected him to do so and then she would really have been in trouble. As he hadn't she wondered whether he had taken what she said to heart. She hoped so. Even the business over Jeff wouldn't seem so bad then. Certainly her mother's attitude suggested that everything was over.

The Wednesday before Easter brought the performance of the college play in which Diana had a part. Madeline was obviously obliged to go and as Adrian was going too he tentatively suggested that they should go together. Madeline agreed indifferently and Adrian was amazed. He couldn't understand what had gone wrong between her and Nicholas Vitale, but from her drawn face and tired eyes something definitely had. He decided not to say anything and hope that this would mean things would return to normal.

Madeline was sure she would not be able to concentrate on the play, but she couldn't back out and as Diana had been so pleasantly reasonable all week she felt it was the least she could do to maintain harmony.

Dressing for the evening she sat before her dressing-table mirror studying her reflection. Her eyes, black rimmed through lack of sleep gave her face a haggard appearance and she was sure she looked every one of her thirty-three years and maybe more. The pallor of her cheeks accentuated the strain already visible in her eyes and she turned away defeatedly.

She wore the dark green coat and went down to meet Adrian when his car turned into the Gardens. Adrian, loving her himself, couldn't help but see what a drawn and weary state Madeline was in and he found himself wishing that Nicholas Vitale could see what he had done.

They drove in amicable silence to the college, both involved with their own thoughts.

The hall was already quite full, but Adrian's seats were on the front row, reserved for them. As they neared their seats, a voice said:

'Hi, Madeline!'

Madeline swung round, her heart lurching. For a moment she had thought it was Nicholas. Instead she found herself face to face with Harvey Cummings.

'Oh! Hello, Harvey,' she said quietly, trying to force a smile. He was with the Mastersons and another young woman, but he had risen from his seat to speak to her. Adrian walked on tactfully leaving them alone.

'What gives, honey?' he asked solemnly, studying her face anxiously.

'Why . . . er . . . I don't know what you mean,' she murmured awkwardly.

'Sure you do. You've not seen Nick lately; I have.' He grimaced. 'He's like a bear with a sore head, but he's not saying what's wrong. I guess I can guess now.'

Madeline's heart turned over at Harvey's words, but sank back again as he continued:

'His mother arrived from Italy today. She's brought some dame with her, a distant cousin of Nick's. I fancy she's hoping to arrange something interesting.' He lowered his voice. 'Honey, ring him, will you? Don't let his mother get her way through circumstance. Nick's going out of his mind, believe me.'

Madeline clasped her hands together. 'Why doesn't he ring me, then?'

Harvey shrugged. 'At a guess I'd say he blames you for whatever has happened; you and that daughter of yours, right? Nick's not proud, but he won't grovel. That's why I know there must be something pretty big digging him.'

'There is.' Madeline shook her head. 'Oh, Harvey, do you really think I should?'

'Sure I do.' Harvey glanced at Adrian. 'Did this guy tell you otherwise?'

'No, of course not. He knows nothing about it.'

Harvey grinned. 'Good. I was gonna punch him on the nose.' He put his fingers round her wrist. 'Honey, Nick's a great guy. Oh, I know he's my best friend and we've worked together for years, so naturally I'm biased, but he's never been like this over a dame before. Besides, working beside him at the moment is downright putrid.'

Madeline managed a smile, and Adrian turned round in his seat at that moment.

'I think you'd better take your seat, Madeline,' he said. 'The performance is about to begin.'

Harvey looked searchingly at her, and she nodded slowly.

'Great!' he murmured, and after squeezing her wrist he returned to his seat and Madeline took hers.

'Several tickets were made available for the executives,' remarked Adrian as the lights were lowered. 'I wonder why your Mr. Vitale didn't come himself.'

'His mother was arriving from Italy today,' murmured Madeline, in reply. 'Harvey is his second-in-command, so I guess he gets all these duties.'

Adrian nodded and the curtains opened.

The play was good, but Madeline hardly realized what it was all about. She was too occupied with her own affairs. Tomorrow, if she wanted, she could telephone Nicholas. But the question was now, what could she say?

Nicholas had not had time on Wednesday morning to go to London Airport to greet his mother and had sent Maria instead in the chauffeur-driven limousine belonging to the company. It was therefore a surprise to him when he arrived back at the hotel at lunch time to find not only his mother awaiting him, but Sophia Ridolfi, too.

He kissed his mother perfunctorily and allowed Sophia to kiss his cheek. This was a contingency he had not bargained for. Not even though he knew how keen his mother was that he should marry Sophia. After all, Sophia was eminently suitable. But Nicholas did not intend to have any match-making done on his behalf, even though he did like Sophia for other reasons.

She looked daintily attractive in a sleek-fitting dress of red velvet which enhanced her fair, delicate colouring. As they had just arrived she was still wearing a silver mink coat and Nicholas was conscious that she was very much the sort of woman he ought to make his wife. She would be the perfect hostess for the social gatherings marriage would prevail upon him to provide and attend, and would always know the right thing to say to his business associates. Rich and affluent parentage ruled out any problems of a mercenary nature and he was sure she would make Maria an admirable stepmother.

Why then did the thought of marriage with her cause him to feel nauseated? He knew the answer, of course. Since meeting Madeline, other women paled into insignificance. It would be impossible for him to live with any other woman now. Even at this moment, his whole body ached for Madeline; her nearness, her warmth, her love. Why didn't she get in touch with him, telling him that whatever obstacles Diana put in their way, she would marry him at once, without argument?

He looked at his mother. She was a tall, well-built woman, with the raven hair and full lips of her forebears. In her fifties, Maria Cristina Vitale was still a beautiful woman. She wore her long hair, wound in plaits round her shapely head and the severe style in clothes which were designed specially for her gave her a regal air. She had tried for years to dominate Nicholas, making him aware of his responsibilities, but without success. Nicholas was too much like her to allow her to dominate him and it broke her heart to see him wasting his life away and not producing sons to carry on the Vitale line. By bringing Sophia to England with her she hoped that he might come to his senses and realize how utterly suitable Sophia was, both to be his wife, and to be the mother of his sons.

She spoke now to Nicholas, and he smiled rather cynically as she said: 'Seeing that you refused to wait a few more days to travel over with me, I decided Sophia should keep me company. She can return to Italy with you.' Her accent was now only slightly accentuated, for she had lived in America too.

Nicholas loosened the collar of his shirt, under his tie.

'Indeed,' he murmured. 'I'm glad you have had Sophia to keep you company.' He ran a hand round the back of his neck and looked at Maria as though hoping she could give him inspiration. She was only too well aware of her grandmother's machinations.

Maria raised her shoulders in a slightly helpless way and he said: 'I ... er ... I may not be coming to Italy, after all.'

'Oh, Nick!' Sophia pouted her lips prettily. 'Why not? You know we have been looking forward to it. I thought it would be wonderful, just the three of us together.'

Nicholas ran a tongue over his dry lips. 'Yes, well,

something unexpected has come up.' That at least was true. 'Look, let's go and have lunch in the restaurant. We can discuss this later, after you've rested. I'm sure you must be feeling very tired after your journey.'

They had lunch and afterwards the two women retired to their rooms to rest without any further discussion of his plans.

Nicholas was glad of the respite and accompanied Maria to her suite. Miss Sykes was dozing in an armchair, but she awakened when they entered. Nicholas usually teased her unmercifully, but today she sensed his mind was elsewhere, as indeed it had been all week.

Maria flopped into an armchair herself and said:

'Well, Nick, Grandmother is determined to make some headway this time. To go so far as to bring Sophia with her! Well! I mean to say. If I were Sophia I would feel awful!'

Nicholas frowned. 'You ought not to discuss such things,' he said moodily. 'You're far too promiscuous.'

'It's only a veneer,' remarked Miss Sykes mildly. 'She's really quite an innocent.'

Maria looked indignant and Nicholas smiled.

'Yes, I'm sure you're right, Miss Sykes,' he said formally, and then sighed heavily. 'God, what am I going to do?'

He turned and walked out of the apartment, banging the doors behind him, and Maria sighed too.

'Poor Nick!' she said regretfully. 'Something serious has gone wrong between him and Madeline, and I bet that high and mighty daughter of hers has something to do with it!'

On Thursday, Madeline had to go to work for the morning only. She felt a bundle of nerves. Through the long night she had gone over and over everything that Harvey had said. She also remembered that Nicholas was due to fly to Rome today, so it was highly unlikely that she would be able to contact him anyway.

She decided to at least try to get in touch with him and

with shaking fingers she dialled the Stag Hotel at ten o'clock.

The receptionist answered but told her that Mr. Vitale was not in the hotel.

'I believe he's gone to the factory,' he remarked thoughtfully. 'You could try there.'

'Thank you.' Madeline rang off and lifted the receiver again to ring the Sheridan factory. She had to consult the telephone directory for the number and a few moments later she was speaking to the telephonist at the factory switchboard.

'Could I speak to Mr. Vitale, please?' she asked unsteadily.

'Who is calling, please?'

'Er ... just tell him it's Madeline. He'll know who it is.'

The girl asked her to hold the line and Madeline waited impatiently. The waiting was not helping her nervous system and it seemed hours before he answered.

'Madeline!' he muttered, in a husky voice. 'Is that right?' He sounded incredulous.

Madeline almost dropped the receiver. So great was her relief. He was still in England! He had not yet left for the continent!

'Yes, it's me,' she murmured in a low voice. 'How are you?'

Nicholas sounded impatient. 'I'm okay, Madeline, why did you ring?'

'I ... I'd like to see you. Have you got time?'

'Sure I've got time. When?'

'Well, today. Any time will do for me.'

'Okay, how about right now? Are you at work?' His voice was endearingly urgent. Harvey had been right. He did want to see her.

'Yes, I'm at work. But. . . .'

'But nothing. I'll be right over.' He rang off before she could object and Madeline sat staring at the telephone as though bemused.

Then she gathered her scattered wits. If he was coming over, it was not very far and she had better meet him outside. She had nothing much left to do so she cleared her desk, put the letters ready for the porter, and slipped on her coat.

'She walked reluctantly to the door of Adrian's office and opened it.

'Is it all right if I go now?' she asked.

He glanced at his watch. 'It's only ten-twenty, Madeline.' He sounded flabbergasted.

'I know, but this is urgent.'

'All right,' Adrian frowned. 'Will I see you this weekend?'

'Come to the flat,' she said awkwardly. 'If I'm home, you know you're always welcome.'

'Very well.' Adrian returned to his letters and Madeline closed the door with a feeling of relief. She had expected all sorts of personal questions about her early departure.

Outside it was a wonderful spring day; warm and sunny with the scent of flowers assailing her nostrils from the school flower beds. Madeline felt it was good to be alive all of a sudden. Her pale cheeks warmed a little, but her eyes betrayed the strain and emotional torment of the last few days.

The red Sheridan halted at the school gates only seconds after she left the building and she hurried down to it and slid in besides Nicholas.

She stared long and searchingly at him, enjoying the pleasure of just looking at him, while he in his turn studied her. Then with gentle fingers he touched the black marks beneath her eyes, and said softly:

'You're a fool, aren't you?'

Madeline did not trust herself to speak and merely nodded. Nicholas sighed and then glancing up the drive to the wide windows of the school he determinedly started the car and they drove away.

They drove away from the town, turning off the main highway on to meandering country lanes, running be-

tween hedges now blooming with all their spring green-
ery and brushing the wide automobile as it droned along.
Wild crocuses and daffodils starred the grassy banks, a
rippling, gurgling stream chuckled its way over smooth
white stones beneath a hump-backed bridge that they
glided over. Madeline felt her fears and apprehensions
melting away in the glory of the morning. Spring was
here, and she was with the only man she ever wanted to be
with. Surely nothing could go wrong now.

Nicholas drew off the road on to a grassy stretch beneath the branches of a massive oak tree, and switched off
the engine. The quietness was only broken by the sound
of the birds and the drone of a solitary tractor in the
distance as it moved leisurely across the fields.

Madeline sighed and lay back in her seat and then
looked along at Nicholas. Now that she could see his face
she saw lines of weariness about his eyes and she said, in a
small voice: 'Do you still want me?'

With a groan, Nicholas slid his arm along the back of
her seat and turned towards her. With his free hand he
caressed the softness of her hair, his thumb moving rhyth-
mically over her smooth cheek.

'Do I want you?' he echoed. 'God, you know I do.'

He bent his head and put his mouth to hers, gently at
first and then with increasing pressure. His fingers encircled her throat and he muttered: 'I could kill you for
what you've done to me.'

She opened her eyes reluctantly and looked up at him
fearlessly. 'Darling you couldn't be so cruel. To yourself
of course. I love you, and I'll marry you whenever you
say.'

Nicholas half-smiled as he looked down into her eyes. 'I
couldn't anyway. You're much too dear to me, whatever
you decide.'

He released her and reached for his cigarettes. He had
got to ask about Diana and he dreaded introducing a jarring note.

Lighting two cigarettes and handing her one, he said
slowly: 'And what about your daughter?'

Madeline drew on her cigarette luxuriously, feeling warm and drowsy. 'We'll tell her today, unexpectedly.' Then she suddenly sat up. 'But you're going to Italy today!' Her eyes were full of consternation.

'Relax,' he said, drawing her back against him. 'I'm not going, at least not today anyway.'

'But . . . but how . . .?' Madeline looked concerned.

'I guess I was going to contact you,' he murmured, releasing her hair from the French knot, by pulling out all the pins and throwing them on the floor. 'Take it down, honey, I like to be able to run my fingers through it.'

Madeline blushed charmingly and quickly released the last few strands, running her own fingers through it, loosening it. 'Is that better?' she asked.

'Much better,' he murmured, kissing her mouth lingeringly. 'God, you know I couldn't have left the country without seeing you again. I'm glad you rang me, though. I wanted you to feel the same.'

'I did . . . I do.' She stroked his cheek. 'And I look such a mess.'

'You're only tired,' he murmured, caressing her ear with his lips. 'Can't you sleep?'

She shook her head.

'Nor can I,' he murmured softly. 'However, that can easily be remedied.'

She smiled. 'I know, darling. And in the nicest possible way.'

He put his mouth to hers again, and for a long while they lost themselves in each other, hungry for a closer contact.

They had coffee in town and arrived back at the flat about twelve. Diana was not at home, although Madeline had expected she would be as the college had closed for the holidays the previous day.

'She must have gone shopping,' she said, taking off her coat. 'Would you like to stay for lunch or are you due back at the hotel? I understand you have another guest, apart from your mother.'

Nicholas smiled. 'Now who could have told you that?'

'It was Harvey,' she admitted, rather shamefacedly. 'I saw him last night at the play.'

'Was that why you decided to ring me?'

'Partly,' she murmured truthfully, 'but I didn't really need much of an excuse. I've been longing to see you all week.'

Nicholas removed his overcoat. 'Good,' he remarked smugly, and she chuckled.

'But what about this girl?' she asked softly. 'Did you used to be in love with her?'

'No!'

Madeline sighed. 'Don't be mean.'

'All right.' He pulled her to him, moulding her body to his. 'She is my mother's candidate for the position of wife to Nicholas Vitale.'

'Oh! So Harvey was right.'

'If he said that, yes.' He put his mouth against the side of her neck. 'Do you think she might be elected?'

Madeline slid her arms tightly round his neck. 'Not if I have anything to do with it,' she murmured tensely.

'And you have everything to do with it, haven't you?' he said lazily. 'No, honey, my dear mama, Maria and Sophia are all on their way to Rome at this very moment.'

'What!' Madeline was astounded. 'But I thought your mother was on her way to America.'

'She was. But when I refused to return to Italy with Maria my mother couldn't let her go alone. Besides, I told them about you.'

'Did you? Good heavens, what did they say?'

Nicholas grinned. 'Well, they looked a bit green at first, but they'll come round. Maria is doing a great job of public relations.'

Madeline buried her face against his chest. 'Oh, Nick,' she whispered. 'I love you.'

'I should hope so,' he drawled, in an amused tone. 'Considering I've already bought a special licence, you—'

'A special licence? Were you so sure of me?'

He shook his head, serious for a moment. 'Not sure at all, honey, only hopeful.'

'Well, your hopes are realized. Are you sure about this?'

'Absolutely. And you?'

'Oh, I'm sure,' she murmured, drawing his mouth to hers again, unable to believe in the reality.

After a few minutes Nicholas put her away from him.

'Go make the lunch, honey,' he said a trifle thickly. 'I'm only human.'

Madeline looked in the refrigerator to see what they could have for lunch. There was some steak and plenty of vegetables, so she decided to grill the meat and pressure-cook the vegetables to save time. Tinned fruit and cream would do for dessert, and after satisfying herself that the meal was under way she returned to the lounge.

Nicholas was stretched out on the couch reading a newspaper, and she smiled.

'I can still hardly believe all this is happening,' she exclaimed with a light laugh. 'When I woke up this morning I dreaded what you might say when I rang.'

'What did you expect me to say?'

She shrugged. 'I don't know. Probably that you didn't want to see me any more.'

'Oh, if you only knew,' he groaned, leaning forward to catch her as she passed, but she evaded him and ran into the bedroom.

'I won't be a minute,' she called, and closed the door.

She washed and changed into slacks and a Tricel blouse, and went over in her mind what she was going to say to Diana. There was bound to be an argument; but whatever happened she intended to be firm. It was no use beating about the bush.

She was applying a pale lipstick to her lips when the door opened and Nicholas stood in the doorway.

'Your pressure cooker is blowing its top,' he remarked sardonically. 'I turned it down, but you'd better check that it's okay.'

Madeline smiled teasingly. 'Darling, don't you know if

it's all right, or are you so undomesticated?'

'I guess I am,' he murmured, shrugging.

'It'll be all right,' she said. 'Am I to have a completely helpless husband?'

Nicholas's eyes narrowed with amused indignation as she rose to her feet. 'It depends what you mean by helpless,' he said, advancing towards her.

Madeline stepped backwards laughing teasingly, but even as she did so she heard a noise from the lounge. She halted and looked past Nicholas towards the door. 'What was that?' she asked frowningly.

'Don't try to put me off,' said Nicholas, smiling and continuing to walk towards her. She backed away from him in mock alarm; she was barefooted and he seemed very big as he approached her.

The backs of her knees hit the side of one of the beds and the impact threw her off balance. With a gasp she fell back on the bed, hands, palms upwards, warding Nicholas off.

'I'm sorry,' she cried pleadingly, but he twisted her hands to her sides as she lay there and leaning over her pinned her to the bed.

'Now,' he said, 'I want a real apology.'

'All right,' she said breathlessly. 'Let me get up.'

'No. Say after me, I'm very sorry, sir, and it won't happen again.'

Madeline giggled. 'I'm very sorry, darling, and it won't happen again.'

'That wasn't quite right.'

'Do you want me to change it?'

'That won't be necessary.' He released her hands and sat down beside her. 'In fact I think I like it better your way.' His voice was dangerously disturbed, as he leaned over her.

'Nicholas,' she whispered achingly, resistance leaving her body so that she was utterly relaxed and yielding.

A few moments later he forced himself up on one elbow. 'And what do you think your daughter would think if she found us here?' he murmured huskily.

Madeline roused herself reluctantly. 'Who could blame her?' she replied, a little shakily.

Nicholas nodded, and rolled over on to his back. 'No wonder she has strange ideas of marriage if you and Joe never even shared the same room. How does she imagine she was conceived?'

Madeline sat up. 'I suppose she's never even thought about it. After all, lots of people have separate beds.'

'I guess so. But I think if I had been her I should have probed a little more deeply into my background; and your background, too, come to that. There was such a terrific difference in your ages. By the way, how old was this boy . . . this Peter?'

'About seventeen, I believe. Why?'

Nicholas shrugged. 'I don't know. I guess I was just curious.' He smiled and sat up. 'Everything about you fascinates me.'

'Really?' She smiled at him complacently. 'That's nice to know.'

'Yes, isn't it? I would like to have known Joe.'

'Why?'

'Well, he seems to have been a genuine character. There aren't many men who would have done what he did.'

'No,' she agreed, sighing. 'Joe was wonderful. When I think how stupid I was!'

'You weren't stupid,' replied Nicholas. 'You were merely very young and very frightened.'

'That's true.' She rose to her feet. 'I'd better get lunch. Diana will be back at any time.'

Her words were interrupted by the sound of the front door closing. Madeline looked weakly at Nicholas, and he immediately rose and walked swiftly to the door of the bedroom. He walked into the lounge, expecting to find Diana, but instead the room was deserted.

He turned back to Madeline, frowning: 'There's no one here.'

Madeline's face visibly whitened. 'Oh, glory, then it must have been her coming in when I said to you that I thought I had heard something.'

Nicholas's face was grim. 'Do you mean to say that Diana has been standing in here, eavesdropping all this time?'

Madeline put a hand to her forehead. 'Probably. Nick, do you realize what this means? She'll have heard everything that we were saying?'

'So what?' Nicholas was angry. 'At least she could be satisfied we weren't making love.'

Madeline shook her head frantically. 'No, no. Don't you remember? We were talking about Joe and Diana's real father. I should imagine from our conversation it wouldn't be difficult to put two and two together.'

Nicholas closed his eyes momentarily. 'God, I'm sorry, Madeline. I forgot about that. Knowing Diana, she's probably made five.' He shrugged. 'Well, at least that solves the problem of whether she should be told.'

Madeline turned away. What a terrible thing to happen! She might have known that the perfect happiness they had known earlier could not last.

Nicholas pulled on his coat. 'I'll go and bring her back,' he said decisively.

Madeline turned round. 'Would you? I don't like the idea of her going off, just like that.'

'Nor do I.' Nicholas smiled encouragingly at her. 'Relax, honey, it's going to be all right.'

After he had gone, Madeline walked over the windows of the flat which overlooked the Gardens below. She watched Nicholas emerge from the building, but there was no sign of Diana. Nicholas looked up and down the Gardens, and like Madeline was unable to see anything. He walked over to his car and slid in behind the wheel and a few moments later he drove off down the road.

It was half an hour before he returned, and when he did so he was alone. Madeline went to open the door on his return and she looked despairingly at him.

'She seems to have disappeared into thin air,' he remarked, loosening his coat. 'I've looked everywhere. She can't possibly have got far before I went out. My opinion is that she guessed we would go looking for her, and she waited somewhere in the apartment building until I had gone out and then followed me so that she was able to observe my movements instead of the other way round.'

Madeline sank down on to a chair. 'So what do we do now?'

'I guess we just wait. Let's have some lunch for a start. She's bound to come back sooner or later. Diana isn't the type to desert her home comforts for very long.'

'Don't you think so?'

'Of course not. Come on, honey. Diana's had a nasty shock, no doubt, but until she returns there is nothing we can do to help her.'

'But will she let me help her?' exclaimed Madeline desperately. 'After all, I'm the cause of her dilemma.'

Nicholas shrugged. 'I don't know Diana as well as you do, of course, but I'd say she was quite able to stand up to something like this. She's not a highly strung girl, she's simply been used to getting her own way. She'll come round. It may even be for the best. She may look on me in a more kindly light now that she knows, or I expect she knows, that her own father was not the paragon she had thought.' He looked understandingly at Madeline. 'Do I sound a heartless beast?'

Madeline managed a half-smile. 'No, I know you're just trying to make me feel better. Let's have some lunch.'

CHAPTER ELEVEN

By eight o'clock that evening, Madeline was frantic. She and Nicholas had combed Otterbury that afternoon in the car, going to the Seventies Club and searching the other coffee bars, but all in vain. There was no sign of Diana. It had begun raining, too, at teatime, and now there was a steady downpour soaking everything thoroughly. They returned to the Gardens twice while they were out to make sure she had not returned in their absence, but each time they were disappointed. Madeline could not think of anywhere else to look.

At last, she said: 'I don't suppose she could possibly have gone over to Jeff's.'

Nicholas frowned. 'Oh, yes, that boy that we took out with us on Sunday. He seemed very friendly with her.'

'Yes. They've been going out together for about three months. It's a forlorn hope, though. She hasn't seemed too sociable with him since he told her he'd been out with Maria and yourself. I don't think she's been out with him since then. Of course, she has had the dress rehearsal of the play to attend and consequently she hasn't had much time. It's certainly a possibility.'

'Okay. Do they have a telephone?'

Madeline shook her head. 'I shouldn't think so. They're not such common things in this country. But I think the address is Poplar Road. I'm not too sure of the number. I think it's about fourteen.'

'Good.' Nicholas started the car again. They had been halted in the town centre. 'Which way is it?'

'It's quite near the school where I work, and of course near the factory, too.'

'Okay.' Nicholas turned the car round and they began moving up the road towards the factory. His fingers gripped the wheel tightly. He felt furious with Diana, whatever her feelings, for causing her mother so much unnecessary distress. All right, so she had had an unpleasant surprise, that did not entitle her to rush away, leaving Madeline without any means of contacting her and distracted into the bargain. He felt like shaking Diana good and hard for her thoughtlessness.

Poplar Road was a row of council houses, each with yellow front doors and white windows. Number fourteen was identical to the rest, except that the curtains looked brighter and the paintwork had been newly washed.

Leaving Madeline in the car, Nicholas himself went to the door, standing under the canopy to avoid the torrent that was now emptying itself over the town.

A middle-aged man, in his shirt sleeves, came to the door and looked startled when he saw the big American automobile at his gate and the tall stranger on his doorstep.

'Yes?' he said uncertainly. 'Can I help you?'

'I hope so,' replied Nicholas pleasantly. 'I understand that a family called Emerson live in this road. Do you happen to know where?'

'Indeed I do. I'm Walter Emerson. What can I do for you?'

'You have a son called Jeff....'

'That's right.' He looked concerned. 'What's wrong? Has something happened to him?

'No. Nothing like that,' replied Nicholas patiently. 'He has a girl-friend called Diana Scott. We're looking for her.'

'Are you? Well, she's not here now.'

'Do I take it she has been here?' asked Nicholas, feeling hopeful.

'Oh, yes. She was here earlier. She had her tea here with Mother and me, and Jeff of course.'

'Of course.' Nicholas tried to contain his impatience. 'Then where is she now?'

'What business is it of yours? She has no father. Who are you?'

Nicholas turned and beckoned Madeline to join them, and said: 'I'm a friend of her mother's. This is Mrs. Scott coming now. Diana has not been home since lunchtime. We didn't know where she had gone.'

'I see.' Mr. Emerson nodded. Then Madeline joined them and Nicholas said: 'This is Mr. Emerson, Madeline. He says that Diana has been here this afternoon and she had her tea with them."

'Did she?' Madeline clasped her hands. 'And where is she now?'

Just then a woman came up the passage from the back of the house. She was a florid-faced woman, heavily made up, with dyed blonde hair.

Mr. Emerson turned to her. 'Oh, Sarah,' he said, 'this is Diana's mother and a friend of hers. They're looking for Diana.'

'Oh, yes?' The woman looked appraisingly at them.

Madeline felt she was mentally calculating what their relationship could be and coming up with all the wrong answers.

'Could you tell us where Diana is now, then?' repeated Madeline hopefully.

Mrs. Emerson pursed her lips. 'I understood from Diana that she wasn't expected home until late. She said that you had things to do.' Her eyes turned to Nicholas. 'She seemed upset about something. Jeff said he would take her out tonight. As it was raining Walter let them take the van.'

Her tone was insolently mocking and had it not been that Madeline needed the information she would have turned and walked away.

'And where have they gone?' asked Nicholas persistently.

'They might have gone further afield if they have a car,' murmured Madeline. 'We've already searched the coffee bars.'

'Was the van in good working order?' asked Nicholas.

Mrs. Emerson stiffened her shoulders. 'It's a new van. Of course it was in good working order.'

'They all run out of petrol from time to time,' remarked Nicholas dryly. 'However, where do you think they're likely to have gone?'

Mrs. Emerson sighed. 'It's possible that young fool is stupid enough to go as far as London.'

'What!' Madeline was scandalized.

Mr. Emerson rubbed his chin thoughtfully. 'Earlier on in the week he was talking about some club that he'd seen when he was in London last weekend. He went up with some friends in their car.'

'My car,' said Nicholas sardonically.

'Really!' Mrs. Emerson was astonished.

'Go on,' said Nicholas to Mr. Emerson. 'Where was this club?'

'In Soho, I believe. You didn't go in any night haunts, I suppose?'

'No,' said Nicholas with a sigh, 'but it's possible he saw the place from the car. We had a good look around.'

'Well, that's the only solution I can think of,' said the man. 'I'm sorry we can't be of more assistance.'

'You've been very kind,' said Madeline, and meant it Whatever Jeff's mother was like, his father was a very pleasant man.

'Well,' said Nicholas, 'I guess our best bet is to drive along the road towards London. We might see them. After all, it's after nine o'clock now and I don't suppose they intend being too late back.'

'I told Jeff ten o'clock,' said Mr. Emerson. 'When he has that van, I always worry. I told him to get himself home before the pubs turn out.'

'What time did they go?' asked Madeline.

'About six,' replied Mr. Emerson. 'I reckon you just might come across them.'

Nicholas looked at Madeline. 'Shall we try it?'

'Yes, oh, yes, of course.'

'Right. Thank you for your trouble.'

Mr. Emerson smiled. 'I'm sure Diana will be all right with Jeff,' he said patiently.

'Yes, I'm sure she will,' replied Nicholas, and with a nod he urged Madeline back to the car.

Madeline felt the older woman's eyes following them and shuddered. Could Jeff really be as trustworthy as his father thought? Had his father been more like his mother she would have been really worried.

Diana looked irritatedly at Jeff as the van ate up the miles back to Otterbury. Outside the van the dreary rain fell faster than ever and she felt utterly depressed. It had been an awful day. First finding out that she was apparently not Joseph Scott's daughter at all, and secondly finding out that Jeff, for all his good looks, was beginning to bore her.

Her boredom had begun the previous Monday when he had romanced on so long about Maria Vitale, but at that time she had still thought she was jealous. Now she knew better. She had gone to his home today because he was the only person she had felt she could turn to. Now she wished she had gone to Uncle Adrian's. When she had told Jeff, in her first wild abandoned despair, about her mother he had actually laughed. Then he had sobered and said that as Nicholas Vitale did not appear to mind, why should she?

She had felt completely alone and desolate and when he had suggested this trip up to town she had jumped at the chance. She didn't know then how she could possibly ever face her mother again, but now she felt a little differently.

'Well!' she said sarcastically to Jeff. 'What a terrifically exciting joint that turned out to be!'

Jeff looked angrily at her, his fingers tightening on the steering wheel. He, too, was disillusioned about Diana and he wanted to hurt her for sneering at him.

'You were keen enough to go when I suggested it,' he said curtly. 'What's wrong? Didn't it come up to your high expectations? I expect a girl like you, coming from such a good home, won't be used to such primitive conditions.' His voice was tormenting.

'Don't be coarse,' she said, looking distinterestedly out of the window.

'I'm sorry. Did I say something wrong?' he mocked her. Then he relented. 'Good lord, girl, at least it took you out of the apathetic state you were in when you arrived this afternoon. Talk about the dying swan. . . .'

'You don't understand.'

'What don't I understand? You eavesdropped on a perfectly innocent conversation. How were they to know that you'd listen in to their discussion? Eavesdroppers never hear good of themselves, surely you've heard that.'

'I know.' Diana compressed her lips. 'But can it be true that all these years, when I thought I was the result of a perfect marriage, that I was really only the result of a furtive scuffle in some back alley. . . .'

'Stop dramatizing everything. You've been doing too much acting lately. You're trying to live your life like some big motion picture, where you're the heroine who is eternally being wronged by the folk around her. Grow up, Diana, your mother is only human. She made a mistake, okay. But don't condemn her for something that could happen to anybody. Good heavens, she might have put you in a home, or had you adopted. But no, she sacrificed her freedom by marrying a man old enough to be her father, just so that you wouldn't bear the stigma of illegitimacy.'

Diana stared at him. Of course, he was right. Why hadn't she thought of it that way? It was true. She did try to place herself as the heroine, whereas actually she usually made a fool of herself. She remembered Maria Vitale and the easy companionship she had with her father. There was no possessive jealousy there. Maria seemed to be glad that her father had found someone he wanted to be with. Why couldn't she be like that instead of spoiling everything for Madeline by her own inadequacy?

'I suppose I have been selfish,' she murmured, sighing.

'Well, why didn't you let them know you were there this morning?'

Diana bit her lip. 'They were in the bedroom when I

came in. I thought at first that they. . . .' She flushed. 'But then I began listening, and you know the rest.'

'And what were they doing?' he asked, amused.

'Oh . . . just teasing one another. They sounded happy together.'

'There you are, then. They probably love one another.' Jeff grimaced. 'Hark at me! I sound like advice to the lovelorn.'

Diana relaxed a little. At times Jeff made good sense and she felt grateful to him for his honest opinion. It was a pity he was so forward in other ways. She was only sixteen, and she had no desire to delve into the intimate aspects of a relationship for quite some time yet.

'Anyway,' said Jeff, 'you ought to be be able to understand how they feel for one another.'

Diana gave him a sidelong glance. 'Why?'

'Well . . . you and me, for example.'

'Jeff, I'm sorry, but you and me . . . well, it's finished! I like you, but I don't want to have a serious relationship with any boy for a year or so yet. I want to finish my training and become a secretary. Then I might have time for that sort of thing. I think I must have grown up these last few weeks in spite of everything.'

Jeff frowned angrily, his profile visible in the light from the panel.

'No girl finishes with me,' he said clearly.

Diana looked surprised and for a moment she thought he was joking. 'What do you mean?' she asked. 'I've done it Besides, Jeff, be sensible, you're going to university in the autumn. You'll have no time for me then.'

Jeff shrugged. 'Why do you think you want to finish?'

'Oh, I don't know, Jeff. I think you're too old for me. I'm still a child and probably the prude you accuse me of being.'

Jeff glanced in his mirror at the traffic following behind and then drew off the road, splashing through puddles into the shade of a copse of trees.

Diana felt herself shiver involuntarily and she said

lightly:

'Now come on, Jeff. We can't stop here. It's a filthy night, I'm cold and wet and I want to go home.'

'Do you now? Well, I'll soon have you warm and then you won't want to go home. You'll be begging to stay.'

Diana swallowed hard. She had got to keep her head. Jeff couldn't seriously intend to touch her. After all, they were on quite a busy road. He wouldn't dare? Right now, the prospect of home and her mother and even Nicholas Vitale was considerably more reassuring than this boy whom she was realizing she hardly knew at all. If only she had not said anything about not seeing him again until they were actually in Otterbury. That was what had started the ball rolling!

Suddenly before she could protest, he pulled her to him, pressing his hot mouth to hers. He held her suffocatingly tight and she tried desperately to struggle free of him. She was frightened and revolted by his lack of self-control and she did not know what she could do to stop him.

'Jeff, please,' she moaned, 'let me go.'

Jeff looked at her mockingly. 'Why should I? After all, you ran after me this afternoon. You were dying for someone to pour out your worries to. That was different, wasn't it?'

Diana twisted in his grasp. 'And I thought you liked me,' she exclaimed.

'I do.'

'Then why treat me like some little tramp?' she cried, feeling angry that he should think this of her and angry at her own helplessness.

'I'm not, baby,' he said, in a husky tone. 'Get on with it. All the girls like a bit of fun. . . .'

'Well, not me,' she retorted. 'If you touch me, I shall scream!'

Jeff looked furious. 'Stop acting, Diana. You won't scream. Besides, it will be quite a new experience. I've never met resistance before.'

Diana was incensed, and in her desperation, she bent

her head and bit hard at the hand that was gripping her shoulder. With a cry of pain Jeff released her for a moment and seizing the opportunity, Diana thrust open the door of the van and almost fell out on to the muddy grass bank.

The road was deserted and she dared not take the chance of a car coming that way. With hasty movements, she pressed herself between the rough twigs of the hedge and crawled into the copse of trees. She could hear Jeff shouting and following her and she got to her feet and began to run. She had a few seconds of freedom and she did not intend to lose them.

The copse was thick and black, and she bumped into more obstacles than she could put a name to in her haste. There was no moon and the rain was still falling relentlessly. In one respect she was glad it was a black night. At least her silhouette would not be so easily seen.

Everywhere was saturated from the heavy rain and the undergrowth soon soaked through her thin shoes and she squelched mud as she ran. In her headlong dash she gave no thought to what might be ahead of her, apart from a faint hope that she might find a farmhouse and help. She estimated she was about fifteen miles from home, which was too far to attempt alone.

She could hear Jeff threshing about behind her, calling her name over and over again. She wondered what her mother was doing and whether she was terribly worried about her. After all, it was after nine and she had not been home since this morning. She regretted so much now, her foolhardy flight this morning especially, and wondered whether incidents like that changed people's lives.

The trees thinned and a moment later she emerged into the open. She looked wearily about her, and to her delight and relief she saw a light in the near distance, only about a field away. The blackness ahead of her showed nothing between her and deliverance and she began running gladly towards it.

Jeff, following behind her emerged from the trees only

seconds after Diana. His anger was spent now, washed away by the chilling rain, and he was cursing himself for acting so foolishly. Diana was terrified and panic-stricken and he felt ashamed because it was his fault. But sitting there, listening to her calmly cutting him out of her life, had infuriated him and he had intended to teach her a lesson. But would she ever believe that he had only intended to frighten her? After this lunchtime's revelations he ought to have realized she was in no mood to be played with and he felt a complete idiot. Poor kid, he thought anxiously, she must be half out of her wits.

He could now see her silhouette ahead of him and he began to run towards her. Then, without warning, he heard her scream loudly and disappear from view.

He halted abruptly, his heart pounding wildly in his ears and a cold sweat breaking out all over his body. Oh, God, he thought, what has happened?

With a feeling of dread he covered the space between where he had stood and where Diana had disappeared. He walked cautiously as he neared the spot, feeling gravel beneath his feet instead of the soft grass they had been running across. Accustoming his eyes a little to the gloom, he tried to see where he was and where Diana had fallen.

Around him now he could faintly make out the shapes of vehicles; large, unwieldy machines which seemed to be either tractors or dumpers, or possibly even cranes. It was difficult to see much at all with the rain still obliterating everything, but gradually, by concentrating on one spot, he realized that below him the ground fell away steeply into what appeared to be a quarry. Diana must have fallen into the pit. She could be dead!

Kneeling down, he lowered himself to the rim of the quarry and shouted: 'Diana! Diana! Can you hear me? If you can, for God's sake, answer me!'

The echo of his voice was muted by the rain, but there was definitely no reply. He repeated his plea once more, but again only the uncanny silence, broken only by the heavy drumming of the rain, answered him.

Trembling, he rose to his feet and stood for a moment, gathering his thoughts, uncertain of what to do next. He had got to get help, and fast, but how?

He looked about him. The quarry was enormous and it was no use him trying to find a way round it and perhaps risk falling in himself. No, his best and only solution was to return to the van, drive to the nearest telephone box and ring for an ambulance.

His decision made, he ran clumsily back through the copse, scratching his hands on branches and falling full length at times into the thick undergrowth.

At last he reached the hedge and scrambled through it on to the grass verge where he had parked the van. Getting into the van he turned the ignition key and pulled the starter.

There was no response.

With trembling fingers he pulled the starter again. Again there was no response.

Panting now, terrified with panic, he pulled the starter over and over again, and each time the engine refused to fire. He remembered suddenly the puddles he had splashed through when he had stopped the van. He had probably soaked the distributor, wetting the points which would not fire until they had had time to dry.

He got out of the van and looked up and down the road. There had been plenty of traffic passing them earlier. Surely some vehicle would come his way?

A car, coming from London, appeared in the far distance and Jeff positioned himself in the middle of the road, waving his arms about wildly. They must see him! They must stop!

The car slowed when its occupant picked out Jeff with his headlights and it cruised slowly up to him, warily, as though unsure of his intentions.

Jeff sighed with relief, and ran to the car eagerly.

'There's been an accident,' he exclaimed, to the astonished man and woman in the car. 'Can you give me a lift to the nearest telephone?'

Nicholas was driving along slowly, the big car's headlights illuminating the road ahead with absolute clarity.

Madeline was on edge. 'She won't thank us for coming after her,' she murmured anxiously.

'My dear Madeline, right now, I'm not wholly concerned with Diana's feelings,' retorted Nicholas. 'She had no right to disappear like that!'

Madeline sighed. 'I suppose you're right. But I'll be glad to find her, all the same.'

Suddenly Nicholas stiffened. 'Isn't that the boy she was with?'

They were nearing a car which was stopped on the other side of the road and a boy was standing talking to the driver. He looked wet and bedraggled, but it was definitely Jeff.

'Oh, Nicholas!' Madeline went cold. 'Do you think there's been an accident? Where's Diana?'

'We'll soon find out.' Nicholas had stopped his car almost before the words were out of his mouth and he walked swiftly across the road to the other car which Jeff was about to enter.

'Hold on,' he called. 'Jeff! What gives? Where's Diana? And where's the van?'

Jeff turned a horrified face on them, hardly believing he was seeing aright.

'Mr. Vitale! ... Mrs. Scott!' Madeline had followed close behind Nicholas.

He closed the door of the car again, and looked helplessly at the driver. 'There ... there's been an accident,' he exclaimed. 'Diana has fallen into a quarry!'

'What!' Madeline had never felt nearer to fainting dead away, but by exerting all her will power she remained conscious.

'Steady on,' said Nicholas quietly, and then to Jeff: 'How far is this quarry from here?'

'Not ... not far. Through that copse of trees...'

'Well, for heaven's sake, what were you doing near the quarry?' cried Madeline, in bewilderment.

'Later, honey,' said Nicholas, pressing her arm for a moment. 'And where were you going?' This to Jeff.

'The van's over there, under those trees. It wouldn't start. I flagged these people down and I was going for help.'

'Yes, that's right,' said the man in the car. He was a big, blustery-looking man, obviously a farmer.

'I see.' Nicholas studied for a minute. 'Jeff, could you give us instructions on how to get to this quarry?'

Jeff looked white and strained in the glare from the headlights. 'Yes, I think so. Why?'

'Well, I suggest you go phone for help, as you had intended to do, and Madeline and I will go look for Diana ourselves. We might be able to find her. I've got a torch in the car. Are you sure she's down this quarry?'

Jeff swallowed hard. 'Quite sure.'

Madeline stared at him. 'We shall want an explanation for this, Jeff,' she said chokingly.

'Yes, Mrs. Scott.' Jeff looked completely cowed.

'Right.' Nicholas was businesslike, taking charge as he had been used to doing at work for the last twenty years. 'Where is this quarry?'

Jeff gave them stammered instructions and the farmer exclaimed:

'Why, it's old Davison's place. Why didn't I think of it before? You'll find it easily enough. It's a massive place. Look, I don't want to raise your hopes, Mrs. Scott, but that quarry is a mass of edges and jutting-out sections. It's possible your daughter might have only fallen a few feet. Just sufficient to stun her and make her unable to answer when this young man shouted.'

Madeline nodded. 'I hope you're right.'

'Anyway,' went on the farmer, as Nicholas was about to go across to collect his torch, 'I have a length of rope in the boot of the car. Would you like to take it with you, in case you can reach her?'

'Sure,' said Nicholas at once. 'That's a good idea.'

The farmer slid out and walked round to the boot. 'I always keep it here for emergencies. Where we live, down a lane that's more often than not a quagmire in winter, I often have to get the tractor to haul us out.'

He handed the rope to Nicholas and then got back into his car.

'There's a telephone box quite near here,' he went on. 'Only a couple of miles down the road. You'll soon have assistance.'

'Thank you.'

The car drove away and Nicholas and Madeline collected the torch and then plunged through the hedge and into the copse. It was still raining hard and in no time at all they were as wet as Jeff had been. Madeline kept blaming herself as they stumbled along. Had Diana not come home and found her with Nicholas, she would never have dived out of the flat as she had done and then she would not have been with Jeff and had the misfortune to fall into the quarry.

The strong beam from the torch provided a good light and it was easy to find the rim of the quarry and to realize how easy it would be to fall in.

Nicholas got down on his hands and knees and shouted:

'Diana? Can you hear me?'

There was no answer.

He rose to his feet, and began systematically searching the quarry with the beam of light, illuminating each wall in turn. As the farmer had said, the quarry was an uneven edifice. Great outcrops of rock spread frequently over the sides, white stunted trees and shrubs, dripping with water, gave it an outlandish appearance.

Madeline shivered, wondering where Dina could be in all that black mass. What if he had fallen to the bottom? She wondered how deep the pit was at its lowest point. Well over a hundred feet, she assumed, unable to judge in the torch light.

Nicholas was methodical and although his slow scrutinization of the quarry seemed to take hours, in fact it only took a few minutes before he said:

'I think I've found her!'

Madeline put a hand to her throat. 'Where?'

Nicholas pointed down, his beam of light throwing a shaft over the unconscious girl. She was lying awkwardly, caught on the branches of two of the bushes, her head hanging limply, her body strung, hammockwise, between the shrubs.

Madeline gave a sigh of relief. She was only about fifteen feet down. Surely she could not be seriously hurt!

'Oh, thank goodness!' she exclaimed. 'She's probably been stunned by the fall, but at least she didn't fall far!'

She looked up at Nicholas. Even in the faint light from behind the beam of the torch his face looked grim.

'Wh . . . what's wrong?' she cried. 'She is safe, isn't she? You don't think she's seriously hurt, do you?'

Nicholas shook his head. 'No, honey, I don't think she's seriously hurt.'

'Then why are you looking so worried?'

Nicholas frowned. 'Look, Madeline, I don't want to say this, but if Diana should come round . . . and move. . . .'

Madeline pressed a hand to her mouth. 'You mean she wouldn't be aware of the danger.'

'Precisely. It's possible . . . I suppose it's very probable, that she won't come round before help arrives . . . but can we take that risk?'

Madeline swallowed hard, feeling slightly sick. 'And what's the alternative?'

Nicholas compressed his lips. 'That I go down to her, on the rope, and tie it round her, then I might be able to climb back up and haul her up, too. If I couldn't get back up it wouldn't matter. I could hang on, and at least she would be safe on the end of the rope if she did happen to move.'

Madeline sighed heavily. 'Is that the only alternative?'

'Can you think of anything else? Come on, honey, we're wasting time. Now look . . . I'm going to tie this rope round that tree over there. All I want you to do is to shine the beam of the torch on me all the way down and make sure you don't dazzle me!' He smiled. 'Cheer up, honey, I'm not in my dotage, yet, you know.'

Before tying the rope round the tree he tied several knots down the length of it.

Madeline frowned. 'What are they for?'

'It's just a help for anyone climbing up or down a rope,' he replied. 'The knots provide footholds.' He grinned. 'All the fun of the circus, lady?' He was trying to lighten her tension and she knew it, and wondered how many men would risk their lives in this manner for a girl who had always treated them with the utmost indifference.

It was a slow business for Nicholas going down the rope. It was years since he had done anything in the nature of acrobatics and he was naturally stiff. Madeline watched anxiously, equally as concerned for Nicholas as for Diana.

He dropped slightly below where Diana was caught, and tried to find a foothold in the side of the quarry. There were no ledges near where Diana lay, but there were quite a few of the stunted bushes, and he managed to lodge himself behind one of them, sufficiently so to release his hold on the rope and enable him to tie it round Diana.

The worst moment was when he was trying to put the rope right under Diana and her body shifted heavily, almost falling against him and shaking his balance. He grabbed at the tree nearest to hand and managed to propel her back into her place and for a second he clung, panting, to the growth, getting back his confidence as well as his breath.

Madeline, showing the utmost consideration, stifled her own immediate exclamation and only the shakiness of the torch light betrayed her inner consternation.

At last Diana was securely tied to the end of the rope. She was still unconscious and Nicholas could see a nasty bruise on her forehead, but otherwise she seemed to be all right. She was very wet, of course, and he felt concerned about the effects of shock in cases like this.

With careful deliberation he climbed slowly back up

the rope, thankful he had provided the knots which helped as handholds as well as footholds.

Madeline hauled him over the edge and for a minute he lay inert upon the muddy surface.

'Are you all right?' she whispered, running her hand over his wet hair.

He sighed and forced himself up on to his knees. 'Sure,' he said, with a grimace. 'Just out of condition, that's all! I really must take up more sports than golf. This shows me in a very poor light.'

Madeline helped him up and then clung to him for a moment. 'I don't know what I would do without you,' she muttered huskily, and he bent and kissed the top of her head, before putting her determinedly from him.

'Now,' he said, pulling on the overcoat which he had discarded during his climb, 'I think we had better try and pull her up. I don't much like the idea of all this exposure.'

Madeline nodded. 'Can we get her up without jarring her?'

Nicholas nodded slowly. 'I think so,' he said. 'The side of the quarry seems to slope inwards a little. That being so, we should be able to bring her up quite gently.'

Even so, it took quite a few minutes to bring up the unconscious girl. She was a dead weight and Nicholas had to do most of the pulling. At last she reached the rim and Nicholas bent and lifted her and took her to lie on the grass beneath the trees at the edge of the copse. He took off his coat and laid it over her, running his hands over her body first, examining her for broken bones.

He looked up at Madeline. 'I think she's okay. I can't feel any fractures. There's always the chance of concussion, though. Do you think we should take her to the car? At least she'll be in the dry then. We don't want to risk her contracting pneumonia.'

Madeline nodded and Nicholas picked Diana up in his arms and carried her through the trees, wrapped still in his overcoat.

Madeline tramped along behind, shining the torch as

best she could, but Nicholas seemed as surefooted as a goat.

They were nearing the hedge when they heard the sirens heralding the arrival of the ambulance and Nicholas smiled teasingly at Madeline. 'Here comes the troops,' he remarked dryly. 'As usual, they arrive when it's all over bar the shouting.'

The next few hours were a nightmare. The police arrived too, and wanted to know all the details. Diana was put straight into the ambulance and, accompanied by Madeline was driven to Otterbury General Hospital.

She came round in the ambulance, but her words did not make sense and although she seemed to recognize Madeline she said very little, before drifting away again.

The doctor, who was with the ambulance, said that she was in a state of shock but that from a brief examination he did not think anything was physically wrong. She had no broken bones and the bruises were only minor blemishes.

Diana was put into a side ward on Nicholas's instructions. He had followed the ambulance in his car, together with Jeff, who had already been partially questioned by the police.

After ascertaining that Diana was going to be all right, Jeff was driven to the police station to make a statement before going home. However, after he had explained a few of the details, the officer only cautioned him about the outcome of this kind of tomfoolery and he was allowed to go home.

Madeline remained at the hospital. There was nothing she could do, but as the Sister offered her a bed she accepted it with alacrity.

She did not sleep much. Nicholas had gone back to his hotel and she was sure he was thinking that after this they could not very well inform Diana that they wanted to get married immediately. She had really postponed things this time, and quite unintentionally. . . .

CHAPTER TWELVE

THE next day was Good Friday and Madeline was awake at six. She had not undressed fully the night before and only had to don her slacks and blouse to be completely dressed. She slipped out of her room and walked along the antiseptically smelling corridor to the Sister's office.

The Sister bade her enter and she went in, feeling overwhelmingly conscious of her slightly muddy slacks, which were certainly not the usual attire for anyone visiting a hospital.

'How is she?' she asked, at once, as the elderly Sister looked up and smiled at her.

'Much better,' said the Sister emphatically. 'She's conscious now, fully conscious, although she may have fallen asleep since I saw her at five-thirty. A nurse is sitting with her and you can go along and see her yourself if you would like to.'

'Oh ... oh, thank you!' Madeline's reply was fervent.

'Come along, I'll show you the way.'

Diana was not sleeping when they entered, and her eyes flickered at once to her mother. She was very pale and the bruise on her head had been dressed, but at least she did not look concussed.

'Hello, darling,' said Madeline warmly, crossing to the bed. 'Are you all right?'

Diana managed a half-smile. 'I think so. My head aches, but I suppose that's only to be expected.'

'Of course.' Madeline looked at the Sister. 'When can I take her home?'

The Sister bit her lower lip. 'Oh, I think perhaps tomorrow,' she said thoughtfully. 'We'll keep her in today, just to keep an eye on her, but I don't think we have anything to worry about.'

'Oh, that's wonderful!' Madeline sat down on the side of the bed. 'Can I stay a little while?'

'I don't see why not,' the Sister nodded. 'Nurse!'

The young nurse who had been sitting at the other side of Diana's bed rose and accompanied the Sister from the room and Madeline took one of Diana's hands.

'Oh, darling,' she murmured, 'we were so worried about you!'

Diana looked a trifle uncomfortable. 'I know, Mother, and I'm sorry, truly I am.'

Madeline stared at her. 'Why did you run away from Jeff like that? You could have been killed!'

'I know, but I was ... frightened. And I didn't know the quarry was there!'

Madeline bent her head. 'Well, you're safe now, and that's the most important thing.'

Diana bit her lip now. 'Mother! It was Nicholas Vitale who got me out, wasn't it?'

Madeline raised her eyes. 'Yes.' She frowned. 'How do you know?'

'The nurse told me. She was romancing over him. She apparently saw him when he came here last night. She said she thought he was very handsome.'

Madeline flushed. 'Did she indeed?'

'Yes.' Diana gripped Madeline's hand hard. 'Was it true? About me? You know I heard what you were saying yesterday, don't you?'

'Yes. We guessed. Nicholas came to look for you.'

'I know. I guessed he would do that, so I waited until after he'd gone before I left the building.'

Madeline nodded. 'I'm sorry, Diana.' She sighed. 'I know what a shock it must have been to you. I don't know what to say!'

Diana looked hard at her mother. 'You don't have to say anything. Jeff said something yesterday which I thought was good sense. He said that you could have had me adopted or put in a home....'

'But I loved you!' exclaimed Madeline at once. 'Right from the moment you were put into my arms, I adored you. I don't think it ever occurred to me, right from the very beginning, to try and stop having a baby, or that I might have you adopted when you were born.'

Diana smiled. 'You did the only thing possible, then, didn't you? After all, it seems that Daddy . . . Joe?'

'Daddy!' said Madeline firmly.

'Well, it seems that Daddy knew all about it.'

'He did. You see, darling. I lived with your great-grandmother and it would have broken her heart if she had found out. Joe needed someone to take care of him and so we made a bargain. He got a housekeeper and I got a husband . . . in name only.'

'I see.' Diana nodded. 'Why didn't you tell me?'

Madeline bent her head again. 'I was too cowardly, I'm afraid. I seem to take the line of least resistance in most things.'

Diana squeezed her hand. 'Like now, for instance.'

'What do you mean?'

Diana sighed. 'About you and Nicholas Vitale! Does he really want to marry you?'

Madeline looked up, her face scarlet. 'However did you find that out?'

Diana grunted amiably. 'It's been pretty obvious for a long time. I was just too stubborn to believe it. I think I have been very possessive. Jeff accused me of being a prude and being a child, but I think I've grown up now. You've tried to do what you thought was right all my life and consequently I've become dependent upon you. Perhaps if I had known that Daddy wasn't my father after all, I might have been different, more independent somehow. As it was, when he died, I clung to you because my world seemed to be falling apart. I see now, that it wasn't that at all.' She smiled. 'Don't look so surprised, Mother, or I may change my mind! I've had plenty of time for thinking this last hour.'

Madeline shook her head. 'Darling, I'm sure you're talking far too much for a girl who only last night was hanging on a tree in a rain-drenched quarry.' She rose to her feet.

'Don't go,' said Diana, at once. 'Please. I'm all right.'

Madeline looked uncertain. 'Darling, I don't know what to say. . . .'

Diana shrugged. 'I believe that there are very few men who would have hauled me out of there when every time I've seen them I've been downright objectionable. I think I might come to like your Mr. Vitale, Mother. The point is, do you think he's likely to come to like me? And what about Maria? I was a pig to her!'

Madeline was so flummoxed with her own thoughts running riot that she could only shake her head in amazement. Then she gathered her senses.

'I'm sure both Nick and Maria will do their utmost to be friendly with you. They're that kind of people.'

'Yes, they are, aren't they?' Diana sighed. 'I shall have to do my best to live up to their expectations.'

'Just be yourself,' advised Madeline, smiling. 'Diana, you don't know how happy this makes me.'

'Take a look at your face!' remarked Diana mildly. 'I have a pretty good idea, believe me.'

The Sister appeared at the door at that moment. 'Mrs. Scott, I think you had better go now. I'm going to give Diana a sedative and you can come and see her later in the day.'

'All right. Good-bye for now, darling.' Madeline bent and kissed Diana's cheek.

'G'bye, Mother,' Diana smiled. 'And do put something more respectable on when next you come to visit me,' she said teasingly.

Madeline walked back down the corridor with wings on her feet. She still could not believe it! But she wanted to, and that made up for a lot.

What would Nicholas say? How would he react? She knew the answer. He would be just as pleased as she was, and doubly so, now that there were no obstacles in their way.

Two months later, the yacht *Maria Cristina* lay anchored in the bay of Monte Carlo. Its gleaming hull sparkled in the Mediterranean sunlight and the water all around sparkled with hidden lights. On its deck all was peace and tranquillity, much different from the teeming metropolis of the Côte d'Azur which could be seen across the dazzling water.

Madeline stretched lazily on the air-bed on which she was lying and rolled over on to her stomach. She was wearing the briefest of white bikinis and her body was tanned a golden brown. As she had often sunbathed without even the bikini she had an even tan all over and even her hair seemed several shades lighter than it had been.

A few moments later, the icy bottom of a glass was placed in the bare centre of her back and she flinched and sat up, looking up indignantly at Nicholas. He looked tall and muscular in a pair of cotton trousers, his broad chest tanned darkly, accentuated by the whiteness of the slacks.

He grinned down at her and handed her a tall glass of chilled lime. Then he sank down beside her, a similar glass in his own hand.

'Thank you,' she said, smiling to him, 'but that was uncalled for. It was freezing!'

Nicholas chuckled. 'I thought it would be the quickest way of rousing you. You looked so contented lying there.'

Madeline sighed luxuriously. 'I am contented, darling. I've never been so happy in my whole life!'

Nicholas's eyes were tender. 'Nor have I,' he murmured, dropping a light caress on her creamy shoulder.

Madeline stared across the water at the principality, the light breeze lifting the hair on her neck. 'Just think,' she murmured regretfully, 'tomorrow we leave this paradise.'

Nicholas finished his drink and lay back on the air bed. 'Honey, with you, I think anywhere will be paradise.'

She looked down at him, smiling. 'That was a nice compliment.'

'A bit flowery, perhaps,' he murmured softly, 'but it

conveys how I feel. Put that drink down and come here.'

Madeline did as she was asked and lay against him, running caressing fingers over his chest.

'I wonder how the girls have got along together,' she mused. Diana and Maria, after the wedding six weeks ago, had flown with Nicholas's mother back to her house in Vilentia. Madeline and Nicholas had flown directly to Naples after spending a weekend in Paris, and had joined the yacht there for a honeymoon cruise among the Greek islands.

'I think perhaps we will find an even greater change in Diana,' he remarked lazily. 'Maria is a great one for reform. She is like her grandmother. Between them, I should think that Diana will have lost all her remaining doubts. Besides, there are a lot of handsome young men in Vilentia, and English girls are always a novelty to them.' He grinned at Madeline's slightly anxious face. 'Don't worry, my mama is very strict. That accounts for Maria's somewhat patronizing air with boys. Italian matrons can be quite something, you know.'

Maria smiled. 'I must admit she's quite intimidating.'

Nicholas drew her closer. 'Don't worry, you'll make it. You have what it takes.' He sighed. 'Tomorrow we fly to Rome and drive on to Vilentia. At the weekend we'll drive back to Rome and I will show you my house. Are you looking forward to that?'

Madeline propped herself up on one elbow and looked down at him. 'You know I am. Our home! It sounds wonderful!'

'It will be,' he promised softly. 'And for a while there'll be just the two of us. My mother has agreed to keep the girls with her in Vilentia. She understands that we need to be alone, just the family of us together.'

'It will be wonderful!' said Madeline dreamily.

She lay on her back, looking up at the clear blue sky. There was not a cloud in sight, and that was the horizon of her future.

OMNIBUS — The 3 in 1 HARLEQUIN
only $1.50 per volume

Here is a great new exciting idea from Harlequin. THREE GREAT ROMANCES — complete and unabridged — BY THE SAME AUTHOR — in one deluxe paperback volume — for the unbelievably low price of only $1.50 per volume.

To introduce the Omnibus we have chosen some of the finest works of four world-famous authors....

> JEAN S. MacLEOD
> ELEANOR FARNES
> ESSIE SUMMERS
> MARY BURCHELL

.... and reprinted them in the 3 in 1 Omnibus. Almost 600 pages of pure entertainment for just $1.50 each. A TRULY "JUMBO" READ!

The first four Harlequin Omnibus volumes are now available. The following pages list the exciting novels by each author.

Climb aboard the Harlequin Omnibus now! The coupon below is provided for your convenience in ordering.

Mary Burchell
Omnibus

An exciting writer, with an adventurous appeal, who discovered her flair for writing romance at an early age. Her true to life characters and the vivid locations come alive, as she weaves the unmistakable Mary Burchell books, which have captivated an abundant following of avid readers.

. . . . CONTAINING

A HOME FOR JOY . . . is offered so kindly, by her uncle and aunt, upon the sudden death of her father. Joy was more than grateful to them, but in the end they were to benefit as much from Joy as she had from them! (#1330).

WARD OF LUCIFER . . . tells of the struggle between Norma, who knew from the beginning what she wanted, and of Justin, who used her only to further his own interests. When would Justin come to the realization that Norma's happiness was the most important interest in his life! (#1165).

THE BROKEN WING . . . a touching story of Tessa Morley, crippled, and her bewitching twin Tania, who had always had everything. Would she now win the love of the temperamental Quentin Otway, to whom success seemed the only thing that really mattered. (#1100).

$1.50 per volume

Eleanor Farnes
Omnibus

A persuasive and most appealing author with an insatiable appetite for travel. Miss Farnes' ability to re-create and share the charm and beauty of vivid locales and spellbinding characters has rewarded her with an abundant following of avid readers.

. . . . CONTAINING

THE RED CLIFFS . . . a charming story, centering on a delightful Devonshire cottage. Alison lived and worked in London, and had no particular interest in the old cottage, left to her on her brother's death. That is — until the overbearing Neil Edgerton laid claim on the place! (#1335).

THE FLIGHT OF THE SWAN . . . the story of young Philippa Northen's release from a mid-Victorian upbringing. Her happiness to find at last, the attentions of an attractive man surrounding her. And then, the threat of jealousy from another woman, which could destroy everything for her! (#1280).

SISTER OF THE HOUSEMASTER . . . tells of Ingrid Southbrook, who came to keep house at a boys' public school, set in a pleasant old cathedral town. Her meeting with Patrick Southbrook, whom she expected to be selfish and disagreeable, and her surprise to find him quite, quite different! (#975).

$1.50 per volume

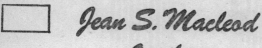

Jean S. Macleod
Omnibus

An author who has endeared many thousands of readers with her books wherein she frequently uses a background of her birthplace, the west coast of Scotland. The authenticity with which she writes of the breathtaking lochs and mountains, captures and takes the reader with her as the story, in its beauty, unfolds.

..........CONTAINING

THE WOLF OF HEIMRA . . . introduces young Fenella and her love of the Hebridean island of Heimra. Her fiance, Val, the new-found heir to the island laird, and Andrew MacKail, with his bitter resentment of them both. (#990).

SUMMER ISLAND . . . set on the lovely Loch Arden, to where Ailsa MacKay returned when her mother became ill. Perhaps the old romance between Ailsa and Gavin Chisholm might have blossomed again, but there had been too many changes at Loch Arden. (#1314).

SLAVE OF THE WIND . . . takes us with Lesley Gair to Glendhu, where the dark mountain peaks of Wester Ross loomed above the glen. She was mistress of the family estates now, and this stranger, Maxwell Croy was intent on buying back the part which had once belonged to his family! (#1339).

$1.50 per volume

Essie Summers
Omnibus

Miss Summers once said that she could fill a book with words she loves. Perhaps this is the main reason why her many thousands of readers have come to know, that when her fingers touch on typewriter keys — the most enchanting characters spring into life.

. . . . CONTAINING

BRIDE IN FLIGHT . . . begins on the eve of Kirsty's wedding to Gilbert when the phone call arrived that was to shatter her life. Kirsty's immediate instinct was to run, blindly away, back to New Zealand, her childhood home, and this led to even more complications. (#933).

MEET ON MY GROUND . . . introduces Sarah Macdonald, secretary to Alastair Campbell. To Alastair, they were perfectly matched, but Sarah had a mental block where Alastair's money and position were concerned, which Alastair worked very hard to remove. (#1326).

POSTSCRIPT TO YESTERDAY . . . tells of how thrilled Nicola Trenton was when her distant cousin George Westerfield invited her to New Zealand to share in the local Centennial celebrations. But Forbes Westerfield was against her coming from the start, and he made his feelings so perfectly clear. (#1119).

$1.50 per volume